QUEEN & COUNTRY

ALAN JUDD

**SIMON &
SCHUSTER**

London · New York · Sydney · Toronto · New Delhi

First published in Great Britain by Simon & Schuster UK Ltd, 2022
This paperback edition published 2023

The right of Alan Judd to be identified as
author of this work has been asserted in accordance
with the Copyright, Designs and Patents Act, 1988.

1 3 5 7 9 10 8 6 4 2

Simon & Schuster UK Ltd
1st Floor
222 Gray's Inn Road
London WC1X 8HB

Simon & Schuster Australia, Sydney
Simon & Schuster India, New Delhi

www.simonandschuster.co.uk
www.simonandschuster.com.au
www.simonandschuster.co.in

A CIP catalogue record for this book is available from the British Library

Paperback ISBN: 978-1-4711-8028-6
eBook ISBN: 978-1-4711-8027-9
Audio ISBN: 978-1-4711-8163-4

Typeset by Palimpsest Book Production Ltd, Falkirk, Stirlingshire
Printed and bound in Great Britain by CPI Group (UK) Ltd, Croydon, CR0 4YY

MIX
Paper | Supporting
responsible forestry
FSC
www.fsc.org   FSC® C171272

TO IAN CAWLEY, BOOKSELLER

CHAPTER ONE

When a sudden illness struck down Mr Noble, window cleaner in the Wiltshire village of Sherston, his place was taken by a younger man who drove a white Fiat van with 'Cleaner Bob' written in black lettering on the side. But there was no telephone number or website.

Cleaner Bob was Polish, people said, although an elderly lady who had been brought up in Hungary insisted his accent was Russian. It didn't matter; he was one of the many Eastern European immigrants everyone heard about, did a good job, charged no more than Mr Noble, made a fuss of children and pets and would clean windows when house-holders were out, content to collect his money next time. His cheerful visits brightened the days of the pensioners in the bungalows and small modern houses behind the hand-some eighteenth-century high street. He was said to live in Malmesbury.

Subsequent police inquires established that no one locally

knew his surname. He took payment in cash – no cards, no cheques, no electronic banking. 'I will become electric, I promise,' he would say, smiling apologetically. 'When I have been established and my bank account will be changed. Until then, please, cash. Thank you.'

When investigating officers eventually discovered the name he used – Kazakov – they were unaware of its possible significance. Reasonably; there was no reason why local police recording an apparently natural death should connect the name of a temporary window cleaner with that of the long-dead Professor Ignaty Kazakov. In 1921 he had been appointed the first head of Lenin's Special Room, established to develop poisons that successive Russian governments would use to assassinate those who opposed them. His name had been revered in Russia's secret poisons industry ever since, though he was little-known outside it and his achievements hadn't prevented him from falling victim to Stalin's show trials in 1938.

But in Whitehall a small number of officials – fewer than a handful – recognised the name when Wiltshire Police reported it. From the start they did not believe it would be Cleaner Bob's real name. He would have left that behind in Russia, unused during his professional life. What puzzled them was whether his use of it was coincidental or deliberate. It could have been coincidental – it wasn't rare and a Pole or Ukrainian of Russian ancestry might plausibly have had it. But if were deliberate, it could only be a sign that Cleaner Bob's controllers were being provocatively facetious. They must have assumed that their British adversaries were too complacent, too incurious, too historically ignorant to recognise the reference. Ninety-nine times out of a hundred they would have been right.

When Bob's van turned into the crescent that morning he brought the weather with him, Mrs Wickens from number seven told the police. He usually did, he was such a cheerful presence. He came a little after ten, just as the sun came out. He did her windows then went to the last house, Mr Johansson's next door. She was just going out to the shops and Bob called to ask if she knew when Mr Johansson would be back. She didn't – she didn't even know Mr Johansson was out. His car was in the drive but that meant nothing because he didn't always take it, even when he was away for days at a time. Kept himself to himself, Mr Johansson. Nothing wrong with that, of course, and he was always very nice when he did speak, very polite. That came from being Swedish, she supposed; his father, anyway, he'd told her. She didn't know about his mother.

She was just going out, had just closed the door, when Bob asked her to tell Mr Johansson when he got back that he'd do his windows anyway and not to worry about the money, it could wait till next time. Which wasn't unusual because people were often at the doctor's or in hospital, being such a lot of old crocks in this neighbourhood.

She thought no more about it until first thing next morning when she went out to water her plants. It had been a while since it had rained, and she thought she'd do Mr Johansson's

3

geraniums in the pots in front of his sitting-room window as well. She often did when he was away and he was always very grateful, always said thank you and offered to do the same, which he never did because she never went anywhere except to her brother in Shrewsbury at Christmas.

Anyway, she'd just done them when she thought she'd take a peek through his window, make sure everything was all right. Not that she was being nosy, but you never knew these days and the house looked as if it hadn't been slept in. Silly thing to say, of course, but it's funny with houses, they look empty sometimes, you can just look at them and know. Well, it wasn't easy because of those thick net curtains and she had to put her nose right up against the gap like a real nosy parker. Which Bob hadn't done, obviously, because he's not like that, doesn't look in people's windows, just cleans and gets on with it.

Then, of course, she got the shock of her life. Mr Johansson was just sprawled there in his armchair, his head at a funny angle. It didn't look right; she knew straight away there was something wrong. Gave her quite a turn, it did. So then she rang the police and the ambulance and all and they came and had to break into his house and that's when it all started, the coming and going. Poor Mr Johansson, he wasn't what you call old nowadays, still in his sixties most likely. But it must've been quick and he probably didn't know anything about it. Heart, the ambulancewoman said, probably in his sleep, so he wouldn't have known anything at all.

4

But he had known. For a few seconds he knew enough to know what was happening to him.

The man behind the alias, Michael Johansson, had been born Mikhail Lubimov, a Russian biochemist, code-named within MI6 as Beech Tree. He had worked in Laboratory 12 of the Operational Technical directorate, a secret facility tasked by Department 8 of Directorate S of the Russian foreign intelligence service, the SVR, formerly known as the First Chief Directorate of the KGB. Department 8 was responsible for assassinations and subversion on foreign soil. During the Soviet era, Beech Tree had travelled overseas as a representative of Biopreparat, the chemical and biological weapons organisation that pretended its business was civilian pharmaceutical and vaccine research. After the collapse of the Soviet Union he continued to travel on behalf of one of Biopreparat's successor companies, with the same role and under the same pretence. During an international conference in Toronto, he was recruited by MI6.

Over the next few years, before defecting, he provided a comprehensive account of Russian BCW – biological and chemical weapons – research and deployment in contravention of international treaties, including the results of experiments on prisoners. During his debriefs he said he had long felt guilty about the use to which his scientific achievements were put, and that it eased his conscience to tell British scientists at Porton Down all he knew of these secret weapons and techniques. Thereafter his ambition, he said, was to live out his natural life in undisturbed anonymity.

He had a great fondness for railways and his absences from Sherston, which Mrs Wickens had noticed, comprised solitary train and walking holidays throughout Britain. He wanted no publicity nor any continuing involvement in his old field. He had seen enough of Russian liquidations, he said, not to risk facilitating the death sentence passed on him in Moscow.

He saw Cleaner Bob arrive that morning, the morning of his death. He was in his armchair in the sitting-room, his laptop open on his knees. He was planning a walk in Teesdale, County Durham, looking for a branch line that would take him nearer to the inn at Romaldkirk than the mainline station at Darlington. The ideal line, from Barnard Castle to Middleton-in-Teesdale, had long been closed, though six miles of it was still open for walking. He would have to get a bus from Darlington. When he saw Cleaner Bob come round from Mrs Wickens's next door with his ladder and bucket, he got up and went through to the kitchen to find his wallet on the table. He owed for Bob's previous visit, having been away. In fact, he had spoken to Bob only once. He did not encourage strangers, especially strangers who spoke foreign-accented English, like himself. Mrs Wickens had told him that Bob was Polish. He had shown no interest. Like many Russians, he didn't like Poles.

He opened the back door as Bob was setting up his ladder to do the upstairs windows. 'Good morning. I owe you money for last time,' he said.

Bob nodded and smiled. 'All part of service, sir.' He settled the ladder against the wall and picked up his bucket. 'May I please have clean water?'

'Of course. Help yourself.' Beech Tree backed away from the door to let him in, there being no outside tap. It had suited him to continue the social-distancing habits of the coronavirus scare. There was peace in distance; he wanted distance from everyone and from the entirety of his past, with one exception. But that was impossible, so he tried not to think of it. Distance was safer, anyway, in every respect. He searched his wallet while Bob stood at the sink with his bucket. 'I do not have enough cash. I thought I did. Perhaps I put it somewhere else. But I can give you what I have. Or will you take a cheque or bank transfer? Or wait again until next time?'

'I can wait. Thank you.' Cleaner Bob lowered his bucket into the sink then reached into the thigh pocket of his overalls for a face mask and small spray can.

'Maybe I put the money in the sitting-room,' said Beech Tree. He left his wallet open on the kitchen table and walked through to the sitting-room, adding over his shoulder, 'I would like to pay now if I can because I may not be here next time.'

Cleaner Bob followed him. 'That is true, you may not.' He spoke in Russian.

Beech Tree turned sharply. Bob was wearing the face mask and holding the spray can before him at eye level. 'Farewell, Mikhail,' he said, again in Russian.

The few seconds of life remaining to Beech Tree were

enough for him to realise he had been discovered but not enough to avoid the concentrated stream of tiny droplets sprayed directly into his face. It felt as if a great fist was clenched inside his chest, gripping and twisting him with a pain that overwhelmed everything. Then blackness, then nothing.

He collapsed backwards as his knees buckled. Cleaner Bob, who had done this before, stepped nimbly around and caught him in an embrace, carefully pointing the spray can away while lowering him into the armchair. He put the can on the carpet, checked Beech Tree's eyes and pulse, and heaved him farther up into the chair. Then he gently, almost reverently, placed his hands one on top of the other in his lap and lifted one leg over the other so that they crossed at the ankle. The leg was heavy and the right slipper had come off. Bob edged it across the carpet with his own foot until it was beneath the crossed leg. Finally he tipped Beech Tree's upturned head towards the left shoulder where it lolled, eyes and mouth open.

He removed his face mask, picked up his spray can, went to the kitchen, replaced the lid on the spray, put it and the mask back in his overall pocket, ran some water into his bucket and went out, opening and closing the kitchen door with his elbow. Then he cleaned the windows.

Mrs Wickens thought it quite a coincidence because Mr Noble, their old window cleaner, had also passed away suddenly, at home.

CHAPTER TWO

Charles Thoroughgood took the call in Swinbrook, the Oxfordshire hamlet where his wife Sarah owned a house. It came at a good moment, just after he had wriggled out from beneath his car after changing the oil and fitting a new filter. All had gone well, the old filter had come off with less trouble than he feared, but he now had to dispose of the old oil. The call came as he stood wiping his hands on a discarded pyjama jacket. He ran into the house and picked up the phone with a clean bit of sleeve.

'Mr Thoroughgood? The Office. I have DCEO for you.'

He recognised the voice of an MI6 switchboard operator who must have served longer than he had. He recalled that voice from his training days and he had now been retired some years. At least they still maintained a manual switchboard. That was something. There had been two attempts to get rid of it during his time as Chief, which he had overruled on the grounds that sometimes agents who rang in needed a person, not a machine.

There was a pause, then another voice. 'Charles? Apologies for bothering you. Martin Manners. You probably don't remember me. I was OS/1 – Ops Security – when you were Chief.'

'Morning, Martin.' He remembered the name but not the man. Ex-army – Guards? Rifle Brigade? Paras? He couldn't remember. He didn't recognise the DCEO designation.

'There's something we were wondering if you could help with. It's not screamingly urgent but we need to crack on with it. Any chance you could pop in for a chat in the next day or two? Today ideally, if you're in London. You still live in Westminster, don't you? You know we're back in Vauxhall Cross now?'

'So I read, yes, but I'm in Oxfordshire. Tomorrow morning?'

'Thanks, that's very kind. Oh-nine-hundred if that's okay? Sarah well? Good, haven't seen her for years. Very fond memories of Swinbrook. Please give her my best wishes.'

It wasn't uncommon for Sarah to know Office people whom Charles didn't. She had never served but had been married to his predecessor as Chief, who had been keen on entertaining.

Rubbing his hands again on the pyjama jacket, he returned to the car, started it, lay down and poked his head under. Gratifyingly, there was no oil leaking onto the gravel. But the problem was the bowlful of dirty oil. Not all recycling centres would accept it. The one that did was miles away and he wouldn't be able to take it in the bowl without spilling it, having no cans in which to decant it neatly. He was tempted to tip it onto the earth in a remote part of the garden where Sarah might not notice. After all, oil came from the earth so presumably there was no harm in returning it. Or perhaps he could pour it on the bonfire and burn it before returning to London that evening. Sarah was at work in London and by the time they came down at the weekend, there should be no trace. It struck him, not for the first time, that marriage and retirement seemed to demand as many subterfuges as spying. Though the consequences were different. He emptied the oil into a patch of nettles behind the compost bin.

'Smarmy,' was Sarah's prompt response when he mentioned Martin Manners that evening. 'A real smoothie. Thinks he's God's gift, though I can't for the life of me see why. He's not even good-looking. What does he want?'

'Don't know yet.'

'Well, watch out. He'd put on a lot of weight, last time I saw him. Wears his paunch with pride. Not that that's catching but I wouldn't trust him as far as I could throw him.'

Martin Manners was indeed large, with dark hair, heavy-framed glasses, a loud voice and a brisk, welcoming manner. He was dressed in expensive-looking jeans, trainers and a crisp white shirt with no tie. His paunch bulged over his brown leather belt, his hands were wide and hairy, his handshake firm and he wore a wedding ring and a Rolex. Charles wore suit and tie, as used to be the norm in the Office.

'Good of you to come in,' Martin said. 'Must be a few years since you were in Vauxhall Cross? Few changes since then too. Denim permitted, ties no longer *de rigueur*, as you see.' He smiled.

Charles nodded. He had read the LGBT notices in the lift and the offers of counselling.

Martin's office faced the river. It was one of the largest in the building, in Charles's day occupied by the director of operations. Martin pointed to a percolator bubbling on a side table. 'Coffee?'

'Thanks.'

They sat in low armchairs by the coffee table. 'I wanted to talk to you about Beech Tree. Russian biochemist. You were his case officer. You ran him until he defected and was resettled.'

Charles nodded again. Beech Tree had not been a difficult case to run, apart from the elaborate security precautions surrounding any Russian case. A clever, calm, focused man who knew what he wanted and had no illusions about what he was doing, or why. Charles had liked him.

'Thought you ought to know he's dead,' said Martin. 'Poisoned, we believe. Ironically appropriate, you might say.'

He described what was thought to have happened. 'Turns out the window cleaner wasn't who he said he was. He was traced to Malmesbury but disappeared immediately after the murder, vehicle vanished, rented flat emptied and professionally cleaned. The Poles have no trace of the name he used, no passport issued in that name. Must have entered and left the country on another. In other words, a classic, old-fashioned, Cold War-type Russian Illegal op, infiltrating an intelligence officer under alias who has no contact with the residency, though they may have provided logistical or information support without knowing for whom or what. Different class of op altogether from the Skripals in Salisbury. That was perpetrated by those two GRU clowns, Chepiga and Mishkin from Unit 29155, their destabilisation unit. Anyway, the Beech Tree op was much more sophisticated, planned long in advance. They went to great lengths to make it appear natural, like a heart attack. In fact, it was a heart attack. That's what he had, that's what killed him.'

'How do we know it wasn't natural?'

'As a result of Skripal, the body was examined more carefully than in an ordinary autopsy. Porton Down was involved. They looked first for traces of Novichok, as used on the Skripals, then they went through the whole family of nerve agents, everything the Russians are known to have researched since Lenin. Nothing. Then they suspected sodium fluoroacetate, a metabolic poison that occurs naturally in plants and causes heart failure if administered properly and is untraceable afterwards. But they've ruled that out too.'

'How?'

'Don't ask me. Something to do with the way his heart

went into spasm. Apparently his cardiovascular system was very healthy, as good as a man in his thirties. They say there has to have been some other external cause. You recruited him, didn't you?'

'Not really, no, though it was credited to me. We had an access agent, an academic who befriended him over a series of international conferences. After he'd given a predictably boring presentation he apologised to our agent, saying, "I would like to have been more interesting; I could have said much more but I know too much." We reckoned that anyone who tells you that wants to tell you more. So the next time he attended an overseas conference I flew out to Toronto and the access agent introduced me. It was really he who did the recruiting.'

'What was Beech Tree's motivation?'

Charles shrugged. Agent motivation was often mixed and the agent's account of it often varied according to when and by whom he or she was asked. 'Mainly guilt, I think. Using his science not to advance human understanding but to make murder easier. That and wanting to start a new life with his mistress.'

'But she didn't come with him, did she?'

'No. He wanted to leave his wife and his mistress wanted him to do that but when push came to shove she wasn't prepared to betray her country by coming with him. She knew that was his plan and seemed to go along with it but at the last moment she pulled out. They were colleagues, you see. She worked in another lab on the same site.'

'But she knew about a new poison, didn't she? So you reported at the time. Something very hush-hush they were developing in her lab, something instant and allegedly untraceable. He knew a bit about it but didn't have details. We wonder if that's what they used on him. Ironic if it was.'

Martin must have done his homework. 'Something like that,' said Charles. 'I can't remember all the details. I do remember that part of her reason for not defecting was what would happen to her family. She had an ailing mother and a couple of siblings. And she was right to worry, of course. When they realised what Beech Tree had done, his wife was turfed out of the marital home and lost her pension. He always felt bad about that. We tried to get money to her on his behalf but couldn't find a way of doing it without compromising her, making it look as if she'd been involved. We still didn't know what had happened to her when I left the case. Is anything known now?'

Martin shook his head. 'No. But our problem is, if it was the new chemical that killed Beech Tree, we need to know what it is, urgently. Before they start spraying it all round the world on anyone they choose. They call it Konyets, which means ending, finale. Something like that, anyway.'

Charles waited for Martin to continue, then said, 'But, surely, above all we need to know how they got on to Beech Tree, don't we?'

Martin nodded. 'That too.'

Skripal had been part of a spy-swop, living openly under his own name. Having been caught and sentenced, he was later released and offered up in part-exchange for Russian spies caught in the US. According to the unwritten rules of the time, there had therefore been no need for him to live in hiding, pretending to be someone he wasn't. Until President Putin decided to ignore the unwritten rules. But Beech Tree was another matter. He had lived very much in hiding, his new name and address known to very few within the Office. After another pause, Charles added quietly, 'Either Beech Tree or someone in touch with him has been unforgivably careless, or you have a major security breach. An insider problem.'

'That's what Pamela said. We're looking into it.'

'Pamela?'

'CEO. Chief Executive Officer.' Martin shook his head, smiling. 'Sorry, Charles, should've explained. Change of designations since your day; no more Chief or C or CSS or sirring or ma'aming, that sort of thing. Just plain Pamela or CEO now. So as deputy I'm DCEO. Felt we needed to make a statement, bring us more in line with the rest of the world.'

Not for the first time, Charles was embarrassed by his forgetfulness. 'Of course, yes, the first female Chief. Appointed a few months ago, wasn't she? I hadn't heard of her until the announcement. She seems to have been commendably quiet since. No fashionable tweeting or anything, unlike some.' He paused again, and again Martin said nothing. 'So what's she doing about it?' Charles asked.

'About what?'

'Your problem. Your insider problem.'

'Possible problem, we don't know yet. She's having it looked into, as I said. Not much more she can do at the moment. Maternity leave.'

'So who is looking into it?'

'Head of security. Actually, Sonia, your old running mate. Pretty near retirement herself now.'

'She was director of operations when I left.'

'I think she was finding it a bit much at her age, too full-on, twenty-four seven. What it's like these days. Opted to step down and go part-time.'

'Head of security is part-time?'

'Only the head. She still has Security Branch working under her. They're intact.' Martin put down his coffee, shifted in his seat and crossed his legs. 'No, but leaving the investigation aside for a moment, what I wanted to put to you was this. We have a proposition. I've cleared it with Pamela. She's in full agreement – sends her best wishes, by the way, says she's always wanted to meet you and looks forward to seeing you when she's back at work. Her background was international aid, you'll probably have seen from the press coverage. Very good, actually, very hands-on, lot of overseas experience, popular with younger staff. But I must stress there's no pressure to accept what I'm about to say, none at all. She very much wants you to know that. We'd both understand if you say no. Absolutely.'

Charles waited.

Martin re-crossed his legs and sipped his coffee. 'Thing is, what it is, what we were thinking is, whether you'd be prepared to go to Russia and make contact with Beech Tree's former mistress.'

Charles stared. 'You want me to go to Moscow?'

Martin put down his coffee, shaking his head. 'St Petersburg. Not Moscow, St Petersburg. She lives and works there.' He held up his hands, palms outwards, like a magician showing he had nothing to hide. 'I know, I know, no need to say it. Crazy for a recent Chief of MI6 to undertake a clandestine op in Russia where he'll be under surveillance twenty-four/seven with his head still full of stuff they'd love to know and wouldn't hesitate to download via truth drugs or torture. But what if we could fix it so that it was safe for you to meet her and pop the question?'

It was crazy. There was no such thing as a safe clandestine operation in Russia, given the resources that could be deployed against the operator. He would indeed be a particular target and Beech Tree's mistress had shown no sign of a willingness to spy against her country. Quite the opposite. But nor had she given her secret lover away by reporting him. That was a crime, of course, which made her vulnerable. Maybe that's what they were thinking. But the Office of his day had never resorted to blackmail. It wanted willing spies, not captives. 'You're not suggesting we should blackmail her?' he said.

'No, no, nothing like that. According to the file, when she decided not to defect with Beech Tree – which was pretty last-minute, she almost did – he gave her a contact arrangement we'd provided and which if activated means that there's someone with a message from him. She doesn't know he's dead, of course. The plan is that you activate it, meet her, tell her what they've done to her lover and ask if she could get the formula or a sample of whatever they're using. Knowing what's happened to him might just be enough to secure her cooperation. Just this once, you can assure her, absolutely. We'd never ask anything else or contact her again unless she wanted to become an agent. Which she almost certainly wouldn't. Though you never know.'

It was plausible, just about. Unlikely to work but maybe worth trying under the right circumstances. However, the right circumstances would surely exclude him.

'Why me? They know all about me, they'll be all over me like a rash, day and night. Better send someone unknown, surely? Or better still, approach her when she's abroad? Much safer.'

'She doesn't travel. Whether by inclination or because she's forbidden, we don't know. Theoretically, travel restrictions went out with the old Soviet Union but there are indications that for some people and some occupations they've been quietly reimposed. As for why you, well, to be frank – I mean, to be absolutely frank.' Martin laughed and touched his glasses. 'To be absolutely frank, Charles, you're expendable. In cover terms, I mean. You're widely known for what you are – were – you're not a clean skin we're trying to keep under cover and you'd have diplomatic protection. You'd be attached to an official Foreign Office delegation. Leading it, in fact. So if anything went wrong they couldn't

19

lock you up and give you the third degree.' He laughed again, amused by the thought. 'And, crucially, you knew Beech Tree well. You can talk about him, say nice things. She knows you exist, he told her about you, so she'll know you're the real thing, not a come-on. He told her all about you when he was trying to persuade her to defect. It's in the file. You wrote it.'

'She speaks English?'

Martin raised his index finger. 'Good point. Not for nothing you made it to Chief, Charles.' He shook his head. 'She probably has some English. They mostly do these days. You have no Russian, I take it?'

'I don't. Maybe you'd better find out.'

'Indeed. I shall do that very thing.' Martin got up and went to his desk, where he made a note. 'You'll think about it, though, will you?'

'I'll talk it over with Sarah.'

'Very wise, the lovely Sarah. Do give her my love. You've landed on all four paws there, if I may say so. Want to have a look at your old office on the way out, for old times' sake? It's Pamela's now, of course. She's made a few changes, put her own stamp on it. But she still has the grandfather clock in there, the one made by the first Chief. Your discovery, I'm told.'

'Thanks, another time maybe. But I would like a chat with Sonia if she's around.'

'Not sure if it's one of her days in. I'll find out.'

It wasn't. Big Ben tolled the hour as Charles walked

back across Lambeth Bridge to his home in Cowley Street. The chimes were audible above the traffic, which had still not fully recovered from the pandemic lockdown. Sarah was at work in her City law firm and would not be home until the evening. There was time for him to get out of town and back. He picked up the house telephone and dialled Sonia's number. He had not used it for over a year but still remembered it.

CHAPTER THREE

Earlier that same morning, in the faint grey light of dawn, the moored narrow boats on the Grand Union Canal lay heavy on the water. Nothing moved; neither the boats, nor the water, nor the hawthorns lining the towpath. Then a hatch opened on one boat and a man stepped out. He wore jeans, trainers and a blue Guernsey, with a dark jerkin folded over his arm. He stood staring at the lightening sky in the east, then locked the hatch. His boat had been painted long ago, mostly green with the window frames picked out in faded red and the name – *Tickeye Johnny* – in white. But it looked solid; there was nothing loose on the cabin roof, the black metal flue showed no rust and the deck area was tidy. At the stern a bicycle was chained to the rudder post. It was an ordinary, unremarkable black bike, with straight handle-bars, cable brakes and the saddle only slightly raised.

The man put on his jerkin, staring east while he zipped it, then unchained his bike, lifted it carefully onto the towpath and pedalled slowly along it. When he reached the road he turned on his lights and joined the early commuter traffic heading towards Leighton Buzzard Station. At the station he chained his bike to the rack and joined the short queue at the ticket office. Most of the other travellers swiped through the barriers with their season tickets.

The man was less than average height, with short brown hair, an outdoor complexion and grey eyes, the left with an intermittent tick. He was thickset but not fat, his expression not impassive but quietly watchful. He asked for his ticket in a Geordie accent. Told it was too early for a day return and that he would have to pay full price, he nodded and produced cash from his jerkin, counting off the notes from a fat roll.

He read nothing on the train, neither on paper nor screen, but simply stared at the passing landscape. He got off at Tring and set off on foot towards town. The sky had clouded over and was spitting rain. He took a black woollen hat from his jerkin pocket and walked quickly for about a mile and a half before turning into a road of 1960s detached houses. It was a quiet road, the houses were well kept, their front gardens neat, their parked cars mostly less than five years old. He pressed the doorbell of Number 29 and stepped back so that he could be seen from the window.

'Okay if I pop up today for a quick chat?' said Charles when Sonia answered the phone. He had to raise his voice over her barking dogs. 'With apologies, of course, for intruding on your day off.'

23

'Don't talk to me about days off. Not my choice.'

'Sounds as if we've plenty to talk about.'

'Did you arrange this with our mutual friend?'

'Our mutual friend?'

'You know who I mean. He's here now.'

Charles ran through a mental list, opting for one of the least likely and assuming Sonia was not being sarcastic in calling him friend. 'Not Tickeye Johnny?'

'The very same. You're not going to say it's coincidence.'

'It is coincidence. Will you pick me up at the station?'

'Tickeye walked. In the rain.'

'Okay, I'll do the same.'

'Let me know which train.'

He bought a *Times* at Euston and sat with it unopened on his lap. Tickeye Johnny was the nickname of an ex-Para, ex-SAS, ex-MI6 surveillance operative and part-time bodyguard. But since leaving MI6 he had become a full-time fugitive from social contact, with no fixed address and no known telephone number. He was known to travel the canal system in a houseboat and was often uncontactable for weeks at a time. His sister farmed in Northumberland and he sometimes spent time in the hill country there, odd-jobbing on farms and stables, sleeping in barns. His sister's address was his so far as his bank, MI6 and his army records were concerned. She took messages but could never say when he would reappear. Pressed, she would say she thought he had a woman somewhere locally, maybe in Carlisle. She suspected there was another down in Bedfordshire, though why she thought that she couldn't remember. Probably something he said, and it may have been Lincolnshire anyway. He never talked about personal things, never had. 'Kept hisself to hisself, liked his own company.' But he was a man, after all, so he had to put it somewhere.

Most people who had worked with Tickeye assumed his nickname referred to the tick in his left eye. Charles, who had got to know him better than most, had once asked if he minded. Tickeye grinned, saying it was a story against himself, a reminder of when he had cocked up with the army in Afghanistan. He was serving with a detachment of Special Forces-trained Gurkhas and had left his section hide one night to recce dead ground in the valley below, where they suspected some Taliban might have taken refuge. It came on to rain hard and simultaneously he began to feel feverish and dizzy. He tried to retrace his steps but was soon disorientated in the impenetrable dark, stumbling among rocks and bushes. Fortunately, the noise he must have made was drowned out by the pelting rain, but his limbs were trembling, his teeth chattering and he was so dizzy that he couldn't tell whether he was going up or down. He knew that if he blundered into trouble he wouldn't be able to blunder out of it. He knew too what the Taliban did to prisoners.

When he felt the weight of a hand on his shoulder, his mouth went dry and his stomach somersaulted. Next he felt warm breath behind his ear and heard a whisper, '*Tickai chah*, Johnny.' That was Gurkhali for 'All right, Johnny.' A

Gurkha in his section had followed him out, and now led him back. They often called British soldiers Johnny.

When his story became known in the regiment, the name, anglicised to Tickeye, had stuck. He was happy to tell the story to any who asked as a tribute to the Gurkhas, whom he admired without reservation.

But few asked. 'People in the Service are too nice,' he had said to Charles. 'They're embarrassed because they think it's about my eye. Not like the army, where I was called Blinker before I was called Tickeye. Suits me.'

His cheerful confession of error was the only chink in the armour of self-containment that Charles had ever detected in the former sergeant. They shared several MI6 operations together when Charles, operating under alias abroad, needed a surveillance or counter-surveillance team. When he could he always chose Tickeye to lead it, which he invariably did calmly and competently. Only once did Tickeye have to intervene.

That was late at night in Istanbul when Charles, hands in coat pockets and hunched against the cold, was hurrying back to his hotel from an agent meeting with a junior Chinese official. It had gone well. The man was an eager agent, motivated largely by resentment of those promoted above him through family connections in the Communist Party. Although his job gave him little access to intelligence, his membership of the Party and access to Party briefings was surprisingly useful. Charles was returning by a roundabout route, agreed in advance with Tickeye and the team so that they could check whether anyone – either Turkish security or Chinese counter-intelligence – was following him from the meeting. He didn't know whether the team would be close to him or far back or whether they would simply have positioned themselves at various points. He didn't need to know and it wouldn't do to appear to be looking. He walked quickly, traversing a network of narrow winding lanes and alleyways populated on a winter's night mainly by the stray dogs and cats that were everywhere in the city.

Or so he thought until a woman stepped out of the shadows and addressed him in Turkish. She was young, her tone urgent and pleading. Normally he avoided any unnecessary contact when on operations but she sounded distressed. He paused, and immediately sensed a presence behind him. Before he could get his hands out of his pockets, a large rough hand seized him by the side of his neck and thrust him back against the wall, banging his head against it.

The face before him was unshaven, close enough for Charles to smell his breath. The man said something in Turkish and held up a knife in his right hand, inches from Charles's eye. It had a broad blade with a slightly upturned point. The man started to say something else when his head snapped suddenly back and he collapsed lopsidedly, as if going down on one knee. Which, in effect, he was. He never finished his sentence.

Tickeye Johnny had sprung like one of the cats from the darkness on the far side of the alley, kicking the man hard behind the right knee and bringing him down. He grabbed

27

the man's wrist with both hands and, turning and using his body as a fulcrum, stretched and twisted the arm backwards. The knife clattered to the cobbles and the man gasped. Tickeye did a kind of shuffle that brought the weight of his body against the man's elbow, yanking it hard and upwards. There was a muffled pop in the dark and the man screamed. Tickeye dropped the arm, picked up the knife, turned to Charles and shouted, 'Go! Run!'

Charles hesitated. The woman was standing in the middle of the lane, staring open-mouthed as the man writhed and moaned on the ground, trying to clutch his useless, flopping arm with the other hand. When Charles turned to run he saw Tickeye pick up the knife, bend over the man and press his head to the ground. Then, almost tenderly and with surgical precision, he drew a straight horizontal cut right across the forehead. Blood cascaded down the man's face as Tickeye stepped unhurriedly back into the shadows, taking the knife.

'Temporary blinding, that's all,' Tickeye explained at the debrief back in London. 'So he can't see for blood, can't see where we go, can't follow even if he was up to it. Lot of blood in the scalp. Won't do no harm, bit of a scar, that's all. Should think himself lucky it wasn't his throat. What he deserved.'

'Did you see what happened to the woman?'

'Disappeared.'

'D'you think she was trying to get away from him or working with him?'

'Working with him, course she was. Bastard like that wouldn't let anyone get away.'

Charles's report of the meeting described Tickeye's intervention and attached a commendatory note for his file. It did not mention the dislocated arm and forehead-splitting. Earlier in his career it would have, when reports were fuller and franker. But by then, not long before his first – voluntary – retirement, concerns about health and safety and duty of care were already drifting across the Thames from Whitehall. Tickeye left shortly after, saying he couldn't be dealing with the rising tide of bumf and bureaucracy, though his boss, the head of surveillance, said the immediate cause was disgust at a Head Office notice offering counselling for anyone engaged in operations. Charles, when later he became Chief, cancelled the edict, prompting the resignation of a newly recruited HR specialist. But by then Tickeye was long gone. He had left a handwritten note for Charles giving his sister's details and the message, 'Had enough. Get in touch if anything needed. Good luck.'

'Of course I accept that coincidences happen, but I don't believe in this one,' said Sonia, as Charles got into her Land Cruiser at Tring Station. 'You're seriously telling me that you and Tickeye haven't cooked it up between you?'

'Boy Scout's honour, cross my heart and hope to die. I've not been in touch with him for ages. Wouldn't know how to find him unless through his sister. Where's he living?'

'Nowhere, as usual. Which means anywhere.' She eased

out of the car park. The car smelled of dog, as he recalled from previous occasions. In recent years Sonia and her husband had chosen to live with a fluctuating collection of canine waifs and strays. 'I was tempted to let you walk, as you half offered, but I didn't want to keep him waiting.'

'What does he want?'

'You really don't know?'

'I really don't.'

'It's about a dead defector. Probably murdered. I'll leave him to explain. And to what do we owe the honour of your visit?'

'Same thing. And matters arising.'

'And you're still telling me this is coincidence?'

They had known each other almost since they had both joined. Sonia had started out as a secretary and had earned rapid promotion. Shortly before he retired as Chief, Charles had got her onto the board, trusting her integrity and judgement above his own. He sometimes got things wrong or occasionally compromised, but she never had. In particular, she had a nose for pretence and nonsense, a quality increasingly scarce in the higher reaches of Whitehall.

Tickeye was sitting at the kitchen table with a brown Cocker Spaniel on his lap.

'Put him down,' said Sonia. 'I spend months training them not to do things like that and you come here and ruin it in two minutes.'

Tickeye grinned as he eased the dog to the floor. His face was more weather-beaten and wrinkled than Charles remembered. His smile when they shook hands showed a missing front tooth. 'Looks like I beat you to it,' he said.

'So you win the right to go first.'

'No, I think Charles should,' said Sonia, picking up Tickeye's empty cup and scooping fresh coffee into a cafetière. 'Having heard a bit of Tickeye's story, I think yours will give institutional context.'

Charles began describing his meeting with Martin Manners.

'D'you know him from before?' interrupted Tickeye.

'Knew the name but never met him. Why?'

'Tell you later.'

He finished with Martin's suggestion that he should go to Russia to contact Beech Tree's former mistress. 'That's really what I wanted to talk about,' he said to Sonia. 'That and how the Russians – assuming it was them – were able to find Beech Tree and kill him. You knew about it, I assume?'

Sonia nodded. 'Is that all?'

'It's enough, isn't it?'

'He didn't mention Grayling?'

'Who or what is Grayling?'

Sonia and Tickeye glanced at each other. The spaniel sat on the floor looking longingly at Tickeye. Another spaniel and a mongrel that was part terrier were sniffing the borders of the back garden. Tickeye nodded at Sonia.

'Grayling is – was – another defector, a recent one, ' she said. 'Former SVR desk officer in Moscow covering Scandinavia and us. Knows all the SVR agents in this country, still in the first phase of debriefing. Tickeye was asked back to be his part-time bodyguard for whenever he travelled or went to the safe house for debriefing. He was the crown jewels as far as MI5's counter-espionage people are concerned. Except that the SVR cupboard of British agents seemed to be pretty bare. The usual handful in defence-related industries, a couple of low-level military sources – though one not so low-level, in RAF radar research – and a couple of militant trades unionists and Labour Party activists, just to show that old traditions die hard. Also one or two in the press and media whom they liked to call agents but aren't really. "Useful idiot" types. So far as Grayling knew they had no one in the heart of government or the intelligence agencies, which makes a nice change. Except.' She paused to sip her coffee. 'Push him away, Tickeye. Once you let them beg they never stop. Except that he knew there's one very sensitive British case, a London case. But he didn't know what it was because it wasn't an SVR case. He thought it might be run by FSB, their equivalent of MI5. If you can remember that far back.'

'Run from here?'

'Run from Moscow, not from the embassy here. But definitely a British case, highly regarded, highly protected.'

'How did Grayling come to know about it then?'

'He didn't, not officially. He picked up oblique references in corridor chat, noticed excisions from a couple of British files, discovered there were meetings which normally would have included him but didn't. Also, he noticed a particular officer was suddenly getting plaudits and promotions for work against the British target. Work which, if it was an SVR case, Grayling would have known about. The officer concerned is called Sorokin. We know him. He did tours here and in Washington. We and the Americans had him down as SVR but Grayling says he's FSB, charged with keeping an eye on SVR personnel and cases overseas. Not normally a case officer, more a kind of diplomatic security policeman. A hard case, unpopular in both the embassies he served in. Not surprisingly. But not a man to let that worry him, according to Grayling.'

'Grayling had no idea of what this alleged British case reports on, which area? Any intelligence requirements which have dropped off the list because they're now being met? He must know all their British requirements.'

'There were no changes, at least none he was aware of. He was going to think about it and we were going to go back over everything with him. Then he rang in to say he'd thought of something, a pointer, something his own boss had said about Sorokin. He didn't want to say any more over the phone, was saving it for the debriefing. But . . .' Sonia broke off to top up the coffees and put a plate of biscuits on the table.

'But then he kicked the bucket,' said Tickeye, flatly. 'Unless someone put his head in it.'

'How?'

'Bit like your friend Beech Tree. I went to his place to pick him up – he lived out in the sticks – and take him to the debriefing house. Knocked. No answer. Knocked again, rang again, let myself in – there are three keys, one with him, one with me, one with Sonia – and found him dead in the kitchen. In a rocking chair by the Rayburn. Dead three days, they reckoned. Warm room. Not nice. Smelt him before I saw him.'

'Cause?'

'Heart, like they said with Beech Tree. Too far gone to tell whether there was any heart disease, he was just about cooked. But middle-aged, smoked a lot, drank a lot, anxious sort of bloke, highly stressed. That was enough for the coroner.'

'Any chance something might show up later? Beech Tree is in deep freeze in Porton Down, Martin Manners told me.'

'Cremated. Done quick.'

'Why – don't they want to test him? That's what they're doing with Beech Tree.'

'Better ask Manners. He fixed it with the coroner. Body was just about cooked, like I said.'

'No pointers – signs of callers, disappearing window cleaners?'

'Nothing known. Never had a window cleaner that I knew of. Police weren't involved apart from reporting the death, nothing suspicious so far as they were concerned. Barely poked their noses in the house because of the stench. He didn't encourage callers but if someone knocked on the door he'd have answered it. No trace of Beech Tree's window cleaner?'

'None. Very clean job. Looks like the same murderer – similar modus operandi, from what you say – but if it was the same man he'd probably have used a different cover. Unprofessional not to. Assuming they really were both murdered. Grayling could still have been natural causes.'

'Of course and we'll probably never know for sure,' said Sonia. 'But you know what I think about coincidences. Anyway, talking of professionalism, there's something profoundly unnatural going on, don't you think?' She looked at Charles. 'Martin Manners tells you all about Beech Tree and comes up with this madcap scheme to send you to Russia but never once mentions Grayling, which happened only a week later. Bit odd, don't you think? I know the case post-dated you and you knew nothing about it, never knew him as you did Beech Tree. But not to mention it, given what happened to Beech Tree and what he's asking you to do, is pretty damn odd. Could hardly have slipped his mind.'

'He'll have his reason,' said Tickeye. 'Something that suits himself. Bastard.'

Charles ignored him. 'Need to know? He could argue I was never indoctrinated into Grayling and had no need to know, even if he's dead.'

'But you very much did – do – given what they're asking you to do in the wake of Beech Tree. You need to know he wasn't just a one-off. As if that wasn't obvious from Litvinenko, the Skripals and other murders in Europe and the Middle East committed by the Russian government.

Quite apart from what Tickeye was telling me before you came.'

She nodded at Tickeye, who turned to Charles. 'What Grayling rang in about just before he died – before he got killed – was something he said his boss said but we don't know what it was. Well, I reckon it was something he mentioned, when I took him home after his debriefing. As he was getting out of the car he said, "I think they must have an MI6 case, someone in MI6. When they told me to review current British casework and suggest improvements, they said priorities were GCHQ and MI5, especially GCHQ. But not MI6. Was not mentioned. Why not? Only one reason, I think."'

'Did you report it?'

'Not on paper. I wasn't going back to the Office so I rang the debriefers afterwards and they said they'd take it up at the next session.'

'Did they include it in their write-up?'

'Yes and no,' said Sonia. 'It was in the first draft, which comes to me for approval before circulation. I removed it. If there's a spy in the Office we don't want him or her – probably him, it usually is – alerted. Nor should anyone outside my department and counter-espionage in MI5 know there's a spy-hunt going on. If there's to be one.'

'Did you tell Martin Manners?'

'No.'

There was silence for a few moments, broken only by the chink of Sonia's coffee cup on its saucer. One of the spaniels was still sitting hopefully by Tickeye's knee, the other lay curled up in the dog basket. Charles stared at it. Let it lie, according to the old saw. Perhaps better let this business lie, too. He was out of it and once you were out, you rapidly became out of date and out of tune. He'd seen it often; capable former officers who, after only a year or so out, still confidently pronounced judgement on issues they once knew and thought they still did, only to sound naive and ill-informed. They were listened to courteously, shielded from their own ignorance, their opinions smilingly dismissed when the door closed behind them. He didn't want to become one. Better not get reinvolved, better still not go to Russia on a dodgy mission.

On the other hand, why not fantasise? Good sometimes came from dreams. If he got the formula for Konyets, the mystery poison, or a sample, and maybe even some hint as to how the Russians were identifying defectors, that would mark a triumphant reprise to a career which, he felt, had ended not badly but merely because it – and he – had run out of time. Such success would be a lasting contribution to the cause, the sort of thing he had dreamed of when he joined. That was where true fulfilment – job satisfaction, in its diminished modern conception – lay. Not in position or pay or honours but in knowing you had made a contribution and were appreciated. In having done the state some service, as Othello put it.

Tickeye broke the silence. 'Who in the Office has access to the aliases and addresses of defectors? Very, very few.

Me, but only for Grayling and a couple of others when I used to mind them. I never knew Beech Tree existed, let alone his name and address. Sonia must know or have access to them all because she's responsible for their security. Plus maybe a couple of others in your department? That right, Sonia?' Sonia nodded. 'Then the debriefers, whoever they are, and maybe a couple in the MI5 section they report to. But they wouldn't know much detail – maybe the aliases but not the addresses because all the debriefings are in safe houses away from where the defectors live. Plus maybe a couple of people in pensions and welfare because they have to make sure they get their money and whatever. And maybe' – he looked at Charles – 'maybe one or two very senior people at the top could easily find out if they wanted. When you were Chief you could have called for defectors' files, or any files, without anyone querying it, couldn't you? Or your private secretary could have?'

'Yes, but not without anyone knowing. It would be logged, there'd be a paper trail. Or whatever the screen equivalent is called.'

'So could Martin Manners have found out?'

'Yes, he could call for any file. But not without there being a record, as I say.' He held Tickeye's eye. 'You suspect him?'

'Yes.'

'Why? Why not Sonia? Or the head of pensions and welfare? Or me?'

'You never knew about Grayling. He came over after your time.'

'But we don't know he was definitely murdered.'

'We do really, don't we? Us three. We believe it.' Tickeye grinned. 'Anyway, Sonia would have done a better job if she'd been doing them in. Wouldn't have aroused suspicion. Don't know about the head of pensions.'

'He's been there since Noah and his ark,' said Sonia. 'If he was bent I think we'd have known about it by now.'

'So why Manners?' asked Charles.

'He's a smarmy bastard and he cheats.'

'We need a bit more than that.'

'I knew him in the army. Not well, he took over the company just as I was leaving to go to Hereford. He was called Golden Bollocks then. Not his real name, funnily enough, but it should've been. Took about a day after he arrived for the lads to come up with it. He smiled too much, always smiling, like he was saying, "I've got the most wonderful pair of golden bollocks."'

He attempted, not very successfully, to mimic Manners. 'Before I left we did an exercise in Wales. Usual chaos, pissing cats and dogs throughout, first cases of trench foot in the British Army since we gave up spears. On the last night we had to do a night attack. Up till then the 2iC – second-in-command – Captain Clark had done all the planning but he broke his ankle and had to be airlifted out, so Manners did it himself.' He broke off, smiling again. 'Complete bloody cock-up. Marched us half the night up and down the bloody Brecons and ended up attacking our own battalion HQ. CO went ballistic and Manners blamed it on Captain Clerk, saying he'd done all the planning. I heard him say it, I was there, and he knew I knew. Nothing happened because I went off to Hereford soon as we got back. Then a few years later he bloody well turns up here.'

Sonia smiled. 'He couldn't have been pleased to see you.'

'He wasn't till he knew I was leaving.'

'But we need a bit more than testicular pride to launch an investigation.'

'It was him who got the Office to find me and call me back. He briefed me to be Grayling's minder himself. But no one ever told me about Beech Tree getting bumped off. Which should have a bearing on the risk assessment, don't you think? Putting it mildly. And when he said I was to be Grayling's bodyguard whenever he left home and I asked what happens when he's at home, am I sharing with someone else or is he reckoned to be safe there, he said no, he's fine at home, no worry about that. Which, given what happened to Beech Tree, is more than a bit bloody odd. It stinks. And then I asked what he meant by bodyguard – the full works, am I packing a pistol, what are my rules of engagement? In other words, do I have to wait for me or Grayling to be shot before I can shoot back or can I take pre-emptive action? I couldn't get a straight answer. All he'd say was, "You must understand we're not normally armed in this Service." With maximum pomposity, you know what he's like. And then I said, "So I'm just a minder, making sure he gets there on time and walking him home to see he doesn't get mugged?" And he said, "That's about it. When he closes his front door your responsibility ends. And don't worry, it won't be for long."'

'It won't be for long,' repeated Sonia. 'Were those his words?'

'Word for word. I didn't think nothing of it, assumed Grayling was getting another identity in another part of the country or only here temporarily, going to settle in the States or somewhere, like some of them do.'

'He may have meant someone else would take over,' said Charles.

'If he's got others who can do this work, why not use them in the first place? Why get on to my sister and hoick me out of retirement and pay consultant fees if there's others kicking around the office who could do the job and are getting paid anyway? Is he trying to keep it off the books? Or make it easier for Grayling to be bumped off? What I mean is, I had the feeling he wanted a bodyguard who wouldn't do much guarding. And then when I went there and found Grayling dead and afterwards it was all hushed up and he was cremated in about ten minutes, I thought, is this what he wanted all along? Is this why he said it wouldn't be for long?'

'And why hoick Charles out of retirement as well, to contact Beech Tree's former mistress?' said Sonia. 'Why not use someone the Russians don't know is a spy? They don't come much more high-profile than Charles. He's going to be under surveillance from the moment he lands. In fact, from well before, they'll monitor him electronically from the minute his visa application goes in. If they grant him one, which would be a surprise to me, given the current state of relations. In fact, I'd be a bit suspicious, frankly. I'd worry you were being set up for something, Charles. More coffee?'

They all liked caffeine. They kicked the subject around but there was nothing new to say. After twenty minutes of repetition, Charles summed up. 'All we're really saying is that we're uneasy about decisions Martin Manners is making, particularly his lack of disclosure to those involved – Tickeye and me – and about his sidelining of Sonia, his head of security. We're also suspicious of his apparent lack of concern about how the Russians seem to be identifying our defectors. Which may be because he, along with MI5, are on to it and don't want to reveal their hands to us. Need to know.'

'Not even to his head of security? She needs to know, surely,' said Sonia.

'She's part of the old guard being seen off by new brooms.'

'Can you talk to the new Chief, the CEO or whatever she calls herself?' said Tickeye. 'You know, Chief to Chief?'

'Maternity leave.'

'So?'

'I don't know her and I'd rather not until we've got something more definite to go on.'

'Only way to do that,' said Sonia, 'is to go ahead and see what happens. Which means you go to Russia. Set-up or not.'

CHAPTER FOUR

Although the operation was in St Petersburg, the letter, the
letter that launched it, was posted in Moscow. Clandestine
letter-posting entailed a week of planning and manoeuvring
by the MI6 Moscow station, culminating in a dinner party
given by the head of station to welcome the new Foreign
Office trade and economic attaché, who was secretly deputy
head of station. For some days the head of station's wife
made very public arrangements for the dinner, with frequent
phone calls about the menu and guest list. On the morning
of the dinner a Foreign Office colleague of the new attaché
– in fact, another member of the MI6 station – rang to check
she knew that the attaché was vegetarian. This provoked a
scrambled revision of the menu and much discussion about
where to find suitable ingredients. The hostess's convincing
panic came as light relief to the Russian FSB listeners who
monitored the phones, microphones and cameras embedded
in all the embassy flats. They were not surprised to hear

that she was about to dash out on a last-minute shopping expedition. She was in a great rush and had announced where she was going; there was no reason to request additional surveillance.

Nevertheless, she acted as if she was under surveillance, which meant acting as if she thought she wasn't. During months of pre-posting training with her husband, she had learned to spot and lose surveillance without appearing to be aware of it, ensuring that to anyone watching she had an obvious and harmless reason for everything she did and every place visited. She parked her diplomatic-registered car and went first to Gastronom in GUM, where she had some successes but failed to find the sour cherries she wanted. She continued on foot towards Gastronomia Eliseevsky, walking hurriedly until her mobile rang. She stopped, put down her shopping bag and reached in her handbag for the phone. The caller was the supposed attaché's supposed Foreign Office colleague ringing to confirm that the attaché would eat fish. This provoked further conversation about what was available and where, during the course of which the head of station's wife moved herself and her shopping bag out of the way of passers-by, closer to the wall of an office building. There she stood next to a postbox, a typical blue Moscow postbox. She faced the street with the remote abstracted gaze typical of mobile users focused on their conversation and unaware of their surroundings. But in fact she was watching for watchers.

'Hang on, I'll make a note of that if you could spell it for me,' she said. 'Not sure my Russian's up to it. Everything's going out of my head these days.' She rested her handbag on the postbox and scrabbled with her free hand for pen and paper. She had to change hands in order to write, switching the phone from right to left and turning her back to the street. With her right hand briefly unencumbered and shielded by her body, she took a stamped envelope from her handbag and slipped it into the postbox. Then she made a note of the kinds of fish the attaché was said to favour. When she continued on her way, no one stepped out of the crowd to slip an official card into the box forbidding further emptying.

The envelope, embossed with the name and address of the Hotel Astoria in St Petersburg, was addressed to a woman in a block of flats in another part of St Petersburg. Inside was a single sheet of Astoria notepaper advertising reduced-price midweek offers. There was a pencilled alteration to the date from which the offers applied and, at the top of the sheet, a pencilled telephone number followed by, in brackets, the number twelve. During his last meeting with his mistress before he defected, Beech Tree had told her that if she ever received such a letter it would mean there was someone with a message from him whom she could visit in the hotel.

Despite being tearful at the time, confused and over-wrought, she had remembered the instructions. She was to call the telephone number twice in five minutes, listen to the recorded announcement but say nothing, then, to go to the Astoria on the evening of the day before the pencilled date and three hours before the bracketed number.

The operation got off to a more tentative start in London. Charles's discussion with Sarah, which he had warned Martin Manners he would have before agreeing, did not begin well.

'I can't believe they'd risk sending you there.'

'But as part of an accredited diplomatic delegation. I'd have diplomatic status. They couldn't hold me for anything.'

'They could hold you long enough to be nasty. And they're nasty enough anyway. You know embassy staff are harassed daily in petty ways, cars tinkered with, flats broken into, power cut off, that sort of thing. They might even give you radioactive poisoning. You've said yourself they're believed to have done that to the Americans.'

'It's only a three-day trip, that's all, and if it helps us identify this new chemical they're using then it's surely worth the risk. Which is pretty slight. After all, if they don't want me there – more than likely – I won't get a visa. And if I do, it suggests they're okay about it.'

'Or that they do want you there so they can do something unpleasant. What does Sonia think?'

'She thinks I should go.' He hesitated. He had told her about Grayling's death but not about Sonia's and Tickeye's unease about Martin Manners and their belief that the Russians had a source in MI6. But Sonia and Sarah knew each other and met for occasional early suppers after work.

It would be bound to come out and anyway Sonia would ask him if Sarah was happy about it. It was the kind of decision that for decades he had regarded as his, and his alone, but marriage, even late marriage, had taught him that domestic harmony carried a price that was occasionally worth paying. He told her everything about the meeting that morning.

'There you are, just as I told you about Martin,' she said. 'Wouldn't trust him as far as I could throw him. I said that, didn't I? And you know how far that would be.'

'But you never had any indication that he was disloyal.'

'You don't need to with men like him. You just know they're out for themselves, only themselves. It's all about them. Tickeye is spot on about him.'

'Selfishness is commonplace, treachery isn't.'

'But why send you? Why not someone else? All this about your having known Beech Tree and that counting with his girlfriend – ex-girlfriend – is guff, just guff. Why not send Tickeye, come to that? He's . . .' She hesitated, ashamed that she had been about to pronounce him expendable. 'He's more used to rough stuff than you are.'

'I don't agree. My having known Beech Tree is the point. I can talk about him to his mistress in a way that Tickeye couldn't. Nor could anyone else.'

'I think you're exaggerating your powers of persuasion. Speaking as your lawyer, I advise you not to go. Speaking as your wife, I'm telling you not to.'

'So long as they accept my diplomatic status, there's not

much that can go wrong. You don't have to take it from me. Talk to Sonia about it.'

Privately, he expected his visa to be refused. Recent expulsions of Russian intelligence officers from London and other Western capitals made it likely. He could then withdraw with honour from an operation he only half believed in. Except that he wanted to get to the bottom of it. He cared about the Service, as his generation termed it, and when he had retired he had felt he was bequeathing his successor and the nation a fully functioning fighting ship. Now it looked to be holed beneath the waterline.

But his visa came through quickly, before anyone else's in the delegation.

'They must want you there,' said Sonia. 'I wouldn't blame you for taking it as a reason to pull out. If you want.'

'Don't say that to Sarah.'

'We've already discussed it. She's reconciled to your going. I wouldn't say she's happy about it, but she accepts it.'

'She wouldn't have taken it from me.'

'Of course not. D'you blame her?'

'Great,' said Martin Manners when Charles rang to tell him about the visa. 'I thought you'd get a quick answer, whichever way it went. They know so much about you they hardly need to look you up or trace you, unlike the others. Open-and-shut case, yes or no. They must think you're

harmless now you're retired, failing memory and all that.'
He laughed.

After some delay the other four in the delegation were accepted. They comprised a Foreign Office interpreter, a newly joined young man from the Foreign Office Russia desk, an older man from MI5 and the woman who headed JTAC, the Joint Terrorism Analysis Centre. They were to conduct exploratory talks about re-establishing the mechanisms for counter-terrorist liaison that had lapsed in recent years, and would be joined by someone from the British Embassy in Moscow. The story was put about that Charles had been asked to head it because he had counter-terrorism experience and because his former seniority would indicate that the British were serious.

'Not that we are serious about cooperation,' said Manners when he explained it to Charles. 'Well, I mean, we are, sort of. Or would be if they were. Prepared to be anyway. But frankly if it's no better than the last time we tried it, when the head of MI5 went to Moscow herself, then it's not worth bothering. The Russians can't seem to get their heads round the concept of sharing anything.'

Two days before they were due to fly out, the Russians switched the venue from St Petersburg to Moscow, without explanation. The Foreign Office changed flights and hotels, only then to be told it would be St Petersburg after all. Next they heard that the embassy official who was to join them couldn't now be spared from Moscow. Someone would be sent in his place.

'Makes things easier for us,' said Manners. 'Kind of them really, almost as if they were doing us a favour. If it had been Moscow we'd have had to invent a reason for you to go to St Petersburg to meet your lady in the Astoria. In fact, the whole delegation is now booked into it for the duration. The conference is to be held there, too. The Russians can be helpful sometimes, so long as they don't realise it.'

'Do we know whether she's taken the bait?'

'No. Nor shall we in advance. Either she shows up or she doesn't.'

'The Foreign Office cleared it okay?'

'No problem here at the London end. The ambassador in Moscow was a bit sniffy but he's come round. He's the only one in the embassy who knows about it, apart from our own people there. They had to know because they had to post the letter. Operation in itself, you know, posting a letter in Moscow.'

'I know.'

Manners guffawed and shook his head. 'Sorry, Charles, I was forgetting. 'Course you do. Spend too much of my time talking to new entrants who don't know anything.' They both stood. 'Oh, one other thing, before you go.'

Charles had long since learned that whatever followed such a phrase was usually less incidental than it was meant to sound. Often it was the undisclosed main point. He sat down again, forcing Martin to do the same.

'Mobile phones, laptops and whatever. You know what

they're like, the Russians. Bad as the Chinese. Anyone like you will have all his comms interrogated at best, tampered with at worst. So we strongly advise you to leave all your own stuff at home and let us issue you with new stuff which you use as a one-off for this trip. Bang up-to-date new kit, free, won't cost you a penny.'

'Sure.'

'And, of course, I don't need to tell you that they'll hoover up any numbers or addresses you contact while you're there. So you need to be careful.'

'I've always assumed they've got all mine already.'

'But surely you surrendered your Office phone when you retired, didn't you? Got yourself a new one?'

'Yes, but they'll have logged all my contacts and they've only got to monitor a few of them to see my new number popping up and work out whose it is.'

'Yes, of course, good point. Hadn't thought of that.'

'Really?'

'Mind you, we've got these super-duper new smart-phones now with extra security. Bit bulky but really good. Quantum leap from your day.' He picked up a thick grey mobile from his desk. 'Does everything but sneeze and fart for you.' He gazed at it. 'Probably that too if you program it. Does more than you think.'

'You keep them on you here, in the office?'

'Keep what?'

'Your mobiles. You bring them in?'

'Have to nowadays, don't you think? Not like in your

day. If you want to be taken seriously. I mean, everyone else does, prime ministers, everyone.'

Charles said nothing.

'But it's only senior management allowed them at their desks. Everyone else has to leave them in pigeon-holes downstairs.'

'That was the case when I became Chief. I stopped it, so that everyone left them downstairs. Unless there was an operational reason not to.'

'Well, times change, things move on.' He continued to gaze at his phone, cradling it in his hand and shaking his head. 'Wonderful things, you've got to admit, seriously wonderful. Things they're capable of. Run your life on them. I do, virtually. Wouldn't have thought it even a couple of years ago but things change, you know, things change.' He looked at Charles as if imparting new and surprising information. 'And what's more they cost us nothing. Get them free from one of our IT contractors. Saves a bit of money.'

'Where did they get them?'

'Well, manufacturers, presumably, people who make them. But I'm afraid the kit you'll be getting won't be as advanced as these. Just a basic iPhone and MacBook or something. All the comms you need and you don't have to worry about what the Russians do to them because when you hand them back we go through them to see what they've done and then wipe them or get rid of them.' He replaced his phone carefully on the desk. 'Seriously, Charles, you should try one of these little jobs. Transform your life.'

Charles said nothing.

He didn't meet any of his fellow delegates until the departure lounge at Heathrow. There were to have been briefings and strategy meetings but the Russians brought the date forward, leaving them only 48 hours' notice. The message from Martin's secretary was that briefing material and discussion papers would be sent to the embassy in Moscow so they could be briefed on arrival.

The rest of the delegation knew each other. The Foreign Office desk officer, a slight pale man of around thirty, was not accompanied by the interpreter as promised but he assured Charles that the embassy would provide one. The head of JTAC was a woman in her forties who turned out to have a PhD in German literature and a working knowledge of Urdu and Persian. The MI5 man was nearer Charles's age, a substantially built, affable-looking man whose brown eyes were enlarged by thick glass lenses. He gave the impression that he had few expectations of the world and was not often disappointed.

After introductions Charles asked if anyone knew of any aims of the mission beyond an agreement to continue talking.

There was silence. The head of JTAC raised her eyebrows. 'We rather thought you could tell us. No one's briefed us.'

'Nor me,' said Charles. 'Where did the idea come from?'

The Foreign Office man frowned. 'I heard about it from my head of department. I had the impression it was an embassy initiative but I couldn't swear to it.'

The MI5 man pursed his lips. 'I was just asked to tag

53

along, waffle about counter-terrorism and make sure we don't commit ourselves to anything we can't deliver.'

'How did you come to be involved?' asked the head of JTAC. 'If you don't mind my asking. Unusual, given your background.'

Charles trotted out the line given him by Martin. 'I did a bit of counter-terrorism years ago and my old office agreed with the embassy and the Foreign Office that I should come along to indicate that we're serious. "Add gravitas", was the phrase. By which they mean age.'

'So can we create our own agenda, make it up as we go along?' said the head of JTAC. 'Could be fun. Much more interesting.'

'Looks like it.'

'*Plus ça change,*' said the MI5 man.

'The embassy may have other ideas,' cautioned the Foreign Office man.

They were given only the most cursory inspection at St Petersburg immigration. In Moscow the embassy would have sent a car to meet them but in St Petersburg there was only a small consulate and they had been instructed to take a taxi to the Astoria. They found a VW Transporter driven by a short unshaven man who looked smelly but wasn't. He drove with abandon, ignoring two sets of red lights and virtually all other road users. Everyone else seemed to be doing the same.

Charles was keen to see St Petersburg. First impressions of new places were valuable, worth recalling when later overlaid by habit and familiarity. Despite spending a significant part of his career dealing with Russians, and despite an enduring love for their literature and the few individual Russians he had got to know, he had reconciled himself to never setting foot in the country. He knew too much and knew also that, even decades after the collapse of the Soviet empire, the FSB took a far from benevolent interest in former members of Western intelligence services. And their families. There were reports of recruitment approaches, physical harassments and crude attempts at compromise involving sex or the planting of drugs.

What first struck him about Russia's most European city was how like and yet unlike other European cities it was. It was 'like' in that the multi-lane highway cut a swathe through bleak suburbs, relieved only by the towering monument to the siege of Leningrad on the outskirts. The makes of car were predominantly German, the drab low-rise buildings lining the highway dotted by lavish car-dealerships. What was most immediately 'unlike' was the ubiquitous dirt and dust that covered roads and pavements and the unwiped areas of car windscreens. The roads were even more potholed than in England, with ruts deep enough to trap and trammel the wheels. It was late March and the waterways were still edged with ice.

'Why is everything so filthy?' asked the head of JTAC.

'Because it's spring,' said the Foreign Office man, confidently. 'They don't salt the roads during winter because it leaches into the drinking water, so they use sand and earth instead, which gets left behind when the snow melts.' He paused. 'Or so I've been told.'

'Don't they clear it up?'

'Yes, but not yet.' He paused again. 'Apparently.'

However, the large buildings in the city centre were clean, the weak winter sun gleaming faintly on the golden cupolas of churches. The Astoria was a combination of Art Nouveau and what Europeans expected of a modern hotel, along with touches they might have imagined to be traditionally Russian. Charles had a room overlooking St Isaac's Square and the soaring, mellow gold dome of the cathedral. His first thought was to ring Sarah, his second not to draw any more attention to her than necessary. His third, as he tossed his own ancient mobile onto the bed, was that perhaps he really was getting too old for this game.

He shouldn't have had it, of course. He should have had his new Office mobile. He was already ashamed at the prospect of confessing to Martin Manners. Privately, he excused himself on the grounds that it wasn't so much memory failure as not bothering, or simply not listening, as Sarah was occasionally driven to point out. Not that that made him any less culpable. He had put the Office mobile and laptop given to him by Martin on the shelf in the bedroom cupboard. They were behind his travelling bag that, through old but now needless operational habit, he always kept packed and ready to go. And when he was ready to go he had simply picked up his travelling bag and gone.

He had realised only when going through security at Heathrow when he saw the head of JTAC take out her laptop. The laptop itself didn't matter so much since he could rely on others to take notes, but having his own mobile was a problem. He would keep it with him, of course, but there were things that could be done to it remotely and anyway they could easily contrive a reason to take it off him for however long it took to download everything.

He resolved to use it as little as possible and on return hand it in to Manners for his tech people to play with, then get himself a new one. No harm done. But confessing his lapse would be the embarrassing bit. He could imagine Martin telling colleagues about it, to raised eyebrows and shaking of heads, saying it was as well the old boy retired when he did, already beginning to lose it a bit, couldn't keep up with modern technology anyway, in fact never could even when young from what one gathered of his career. There really was no room for people like that in the Office any more.

He checked that the phone was still charged and put it in his pocket. He had suggested to the others that they meet in the bar before dinner, when they were also supposed to rendezvous with the embassy interpreter. They had been told to expect a man called Ian but found instead a tall young woman called Moira with freckles and masses of frizzy red hair.

'You're lumbered with me, I'm afraid,' she said. 'Drawn the short straw. The embassy's stretched to breaking point and Ian has been hauled off to this ministerial trade delegation.'

'You do speak Russian, don't you?' asked Charles.

'Not to interpreter standard but enough to get by, I hope. That's the plan, anyway.'

'What's the rest of the plan? The agenda. We haven't seen anything yet.'

'God, you haven't? You really haven't? Well, nor have I. I was only told I was going at the last minute, just had time to get the train. I assumed you would have it.'

'None of us has seen it. We're beginning to doubt there ever was one.'

Everyone laughed except the Foreign Office man. 'We understood the embassy had one,' he said. 'It hadn't been copied to London by the time I left. I assumed Ian would bring it.'

Moira shook her hair. 'No one said anything to me about it. Typical. But don't worry, I'll get on to the duty officer in Moscow. They can email it overnight. They'll have to, we've got our first session at nine tomorrow.'

The MI5 man smiled. 'How I shall miss British bureaucracy when I retire. We tell ourselves we have a genius for improvisation but really it's just that most of the time we have no choice.'

Dinner, on Moira's advice, was traditional Russian stroganoff. It was relaxed and amicable, as with any group of public servants dining at taxpayers' expense, united in common purpose and undistracted by pressure of work. They all deferred to Charles to such an extent that he worried they saw him as a harmless old buffer who had to be humoured. Once back in his room he again resisted the temptation to ring Sarah; she was bound to ask how things were and he wanted neither to dissemble nor to reveal British bureaucratic inadequacy. He knew he wouldn't relax until the real purpose of his visit, the meeting with Beech Tree's mistress, was achieved. It was scheduled for eight o'clock the following evening. Although there had been no response from her. The last he had heard from Martin Manners was that Moscow station would find a way of getting messages to him, if there were any. He was not to attempt to contact them.

At breakfast Moira told them that the embassy had emailed overnight saying they knew no more about the conference than that it was in their hotel, starting at ten. 'Not nine, as I was told before leaving,' she said. 'And still no agenda. The duty officer spoke to Ian, who said he understood from London that the Russians were providing one but no one has seen it.'

'What – without even asking us what we want on it?' said the head of JTAC.

'True to form, I'm afraid. They only ever talk about what they want to talk about. Not interested in anything we say.'

'Unless they want something,' said the MI5 man.

At ten to ten Charles went to reception to ask about meeting rooms. Moira followed him, uninvited. 'I'm MOS/1,' she whispered. 'Can we have a chat later?'

That meant she must be the outgoing deputy head of

station. Charles nodded without looking at her as the receptionist turned to them. Moira gave the name of the delegation in Russian and asked for the meeting room. The receptionist looked at her screen, then got up and went to her colleague. There was a muted conversation followed by the sound of a buzzer. The office door behind them opened and an older woman emerged. There was further muted conversation, then all three looked at the screen. The woman returned to her office and picked up the phone. The receptionist smiled and apologised for keeping them, in English.

They were still waiting at two minutes to ten when a dozen suited and sombre-looking men entered reception. A waiting concierge immediately greeted them and shepherded them upstairs. 'That's them,' said Moira. 'Must be, you can always tell. I suggest we just tag along behind them rather than wait for an answer here.'

They collected the others. 'Why couldn't they just tell us where to go?' asked the head of JTAC.

'Probably because the room's booked in the name of the *organi* – one of the other organs of state security, probably the FSB – and they didn't know what they were allowed to say about it,' said Moira. 'So they said nothing. Always the safest policy here.'

'Will they have bugged our rooms?'

'Bound to,' said the MI5 man.

'Well, good luck to them with that,' said the head of JTAC. 'Anyone listening will die of boredom. In my case, anyway.'

'Maybe you should sing for them tonight,' said the

Foreign Office man. 'Maybe we all should. Let them think we're really a choir.'

The conference room was an elaborate rococo creation with a long polished table surrounded by chairs, and tea, coffee, drinks and fruit on a smaller table at one end. Place cards indicated that the Russian delegation would occupy one side and both ends of the long table, with the smaller British party spread out along the other side. The spaces between them were wide enough to render discreet consultations impossible. The British cards were named, the Russian ones merely numbered. The Russian delegation made immediately for the food and drink table. They were mostly middle-aged, with the exception of a slim young man with heavy-framed glasses who turned out to be the interpreter and an older man, tall with iron-grey hair, who stood slightly apart, smoking and sipping coffee.

Moira and the interpreter spoke, after which she walked swiftly to her seat, indicating to the rest of the British delegation to do the same before any of them had had time to get through the Russians to the provisions table. The interpreter stood with his hands together, as in prayer. 'Ladies and gentlemen, let us be seated,' he said in clear American English.

Charles took his place at the middle of the delegation, aware of being watched by the tall older man. He had pendulous ears and bristly grey eyebrows. His eyes were blue-grey and his pale, deeply lined features looked as if a studied lack of expression had been chiselled into them.

Introductions followed. The interpreter introduced each of the Russians, describing them as officials of the Ministry of Interior with no indication of their function. The exception was the man with the pendulous ears, whom he named as Colonel Kirill Sergeyevich Sorokin 'of our intelligence service'. Charles remembered the name from his briefing by Sonia and Tickeye. It could be coincidence, but it was most likely that this was the man reportedly praised and promoted for his work against the British target.

The British were left to introduce themselves. Taking his cue from what was said of the colonel, Charles introduced himself as 'formerly of the British intelligence service'. The interpreter then took a folder from his briefcase and read aloud in English a history of intelligence cooperation between Russia and Britain, beginning with liaison between the Tsarist Okhrana and the Metropolitan Police Special Branch in operations against anarchist terrorists before the First World War. He then described liaison with MI6 and the British War Office until 1917, then jumped to cooperation in work against the Fascist enemy in what he called the Great Patriotic War of 1941 to 1945. There was then another jump up to the 1990s when the two countries were described as united in the struggle against Islamist terrorism as exemplified by the terrorist insurgency in Chechnya, which was now 'happily concluded'.

This took about fifteen minutes. When he began, most of the Russians took out their mobiles, holding them just below the level of the table. The British tried to look politely interested, the Foreign Office man taking the odd note. Charles was spared the prospect of having to respond in kind by the interpreter's announcement that they would all now break for coffee.

'Wonderful use of time and taxpayers' money,' whispered the head of JTAC as she hurried to the other table ahead of the Russians. 'No mention of an agenda. What d'you think's next in this fruitful exchange?'

'How about you describing the formation and structure of JTAC?'

'You're joking.'

The tall colonel appeared at Charles's shoulder. 'Sir Thoroughgood, may I introduce myself?' His English was careful but clear.

They shook hands. The head of JTAC left them. 'Mister,' said Charles. 'Or Charles.'

'I am sorry for you. I had thought the Chief of MI6 was always a sir?'

'It used to be automatic but things are done differently now.' He was accustomed to occasional, usually more oblique, questions about his lack of a K, as knighthoods were known. All his predecessors had been knighted, mostly while still serving. The current heads of MI5 and GCHQ had been. Three former heads of MI5 had been elevated to the peerage. So far as he knew, there had been no change in the system by which government departments were allocated a share of honours for their own staff, the senior ones mostly according to precedent, the more junior because they deserved it. Charles was puzzled at being overlooked. He had not presided over any obvious disasters and no one in Whitehall had hinted at any problems with his performance. He could, however, imagine there might be questions arising from various episodes from his past, such as his role in the death of his predecessor and his rapid marriage to his predecessor's widow. Or his role in the police shooting of his illegitimate son. Or his own shooting of a renegade colleague. Or his part in the suicide of the man he had chosen to succeed him. Enough, perhaps, to alarm the honours committee, although nothing culpable, let alone criminal, and none of it – or not much of it – pushed under the carpet. He did not greatly mind the lack of recognition – there was almost more distinction in being the exception – but he was curious. So was Sarah, who seemed to resent it more than he. Despite her urging, he had never asked, knowing it was a question that would never be answered. Nor, nowadays, did he know whom to ask.

'Unfortunate for you that the system changes when it is your turn.' The colonel smiled, deepening his facial crevices and showing an incomplete set of nicotine-stained teeth. 'And now you have this job. This little job.'

'Not a job. I was merely asked to help with this delegation.'

'But a big change for you? Such a little delegation?'

Charles smiled. 'Perhaps a sign that our government regards relations with yours as sufficiently important to merit the deployment of retired senior officials.'

The colonel smiled.

The interpreter clapped his hands. 'Please, we will continue. Now we tell you the history of our operations in Chechnya and after lunch you describe the organisation of Joint Terrorism Analysis Centre.'

A screen had been erected during the coffee break and the interpreter's talk was accompanied by a slideshow of cheerful Chechens, resolute Russian soldiers and graphic atrocities perpetrated by dead Chechens. It was accompanied by tables of facts and figures about the uprising. When they broke for lunch the provisions table had been replenished with drinks and sandwiches.

'You didn't put them up to that, did you?' whispered the head of JTAC to Charles as they moved towards it. 'I've got masses of slides and wiring diagrams for the most boring talk in the world about JTAC but none of them here.'

'I didn't, I promise. All their own doing.'

She smiled disbelievingly. 'All right if I look to you for an authoritative hour or so on the MI6 contribution to JTAC?'

They helped themselves to wine and sandwiches, which were mainly seafood. There was wine but no soft drinks. The wine was good. 'From the Caucasus,' said Moira. 'One of the many secrets of this country – they grow really good wine.'

There was no mixing over lunch. It was not clear whether any of the Russians, apart from the interpreter and Colonel Sorokin, spoke English. Throughout the interpreter's talk they had been intent on their mobiles and throughout lunch they were intent on food and drink, though they managed to talk unceasingly while chewing and swallowing and – most of them – smoking. The colonel and the interpreter stood apart, talking to each other.

'I'd forgotten what smoke-filled rooms were like,' said the MI5 man. 'Takes me back to when I joined.'

They moved away towards a window. 'D'you know anything about our representative from the organs of state security?' asked Charles. He couldn't let on what he'd heard already from Sonia and Tickeye.

'Not really but the name rings distant bells. I think someone of that name did a tour in London about twenty years ago.'

'His English is good.'

'Probably the same then. In which case we'd normally say probably SVR, the old KGB First Chief Directorate, the overseas bit, equivalent of your old service. If he were FSB, the old Second Chief Directorate, equivalent of my service, he probably wouldn't have such good English and wouldn't want to be seen talking to you.' He shrugged. 'But not necessarily. There are always exceptions. And if he's here as a minder that's very much an FSB role. Unless he's hoping you might want to talk to him, seeking to supplement your pension?'

The sandwiches were rapidly finished and the wine as rapidly replenished, along with a couple of bottles of vodka. Moira drifted over. 'Not sure how long this is going on for. Would you like me to suggest we resume before we're all plastered?'

'Give them a few more minutes. It'll help them sleep through our talks. Fewer awkward questions.'

'May as well have another sip ourselves, then,' said the MI5 man. He took their glasses over to the serving table.

'Is this typical of delegation meetings?' Charles asked Moira.

'Can't say really, I've not been to many. Not often allowed out on my own.' She looked directly at him, lowering her voice. 'We think your friend has now responded. Someone rang the Finnish number Beech Tree left her twice in five minutes.'

'How will she know my room? It's not the number given in the message.'

'No, that's number eighteen. She's not coming to your room anyway. We assume that will be bugged, audio and visual, the whole works, given who you are.'

He nodded as if what she'd said was obvious. It was, but he hadn't thought about it, not yet. Further evidence that he was too long out of it.

'The room you'll use is not yours but another that's been taken in someone else's name, nothing to do with us or the delegation. Someone who's not going to occupy it. I've got the key card and I'll be there first. You join me there. The number eighteen she's been given is at the end of the corridor round a corner so the door isn't overlooked by any of the others. I'll be there to intercept her and redirect her to our room. She knows not to ask at reception but to go straight up.'

'You might be overheard.'

'I don't have to say anything. I just lead her to our room. Same position one floor above.'

The afternoon session was shorter. The head of JTAC gave a succinct account of the formation and functioning of her interdepartmental analysis unit, ending by saying she was sure Charles would welcome the chance to give his views on current and future trends in international terrorism. She couldn't entirely suppress a smile as she said it. Neither could Charles as he got to his feet. The Russians looked up only briefly from their phone screens at the change of speaker. Somewhat to his own surprise, he found he was able to waffle for about thirty minutes on the short lives of most terrorist movements, the reasons why few persisted for decades, their problems with inter-generational transfer, the advantages and disadvantages of negotiation, and the reasons why governments usually won. There were no questions.

The session concluded with another address from the interpreter, this time about how in Syria Russia had borne the brunt of the free world's struggle against Islamist extremism. He reminded them that they were all to meet downstairs for dinner at seven, adding, 'Now you are free.'

Light was fading but it was not yet dark. Charles decided to use his freedom to sample the streets of St Petersburg. A sign in reception warned African guests against venturing out alone at night. He reckoned he should be safe enough in his ancient army-issue overcoat, brown leather gloves and Donegal tweed hat bought during an operational trip to Dublin. Frequent trips overseas under various covers had persuaded him that, in countries where it was foolhardy to try to pass as a native, it was better to go to the other extreme and appear quintessentially – if in fact far from typically – British. Acting the innocent abroad, the harmless, guileless, slightly clueless, unthreatening, middle-class Englishman, encouraged suspicious officials to relax. It helped them feel they were properly in charge and quite often they became unintentionally helpful.

There was a chill wind and the pavements were busy with huddled, muffled people, all wearing hats. Shops were closing and those still open were difficult to see into, their fronts seemingly designed to discourage window-shopping. He walked slowly, pausing twice, the first time to watch three adolescent boys and a girl trotting bare-backed horses round St Isaac's Square, laughingly heedless of traffic. His second pause was to gaze upon the severe, almost Stalinist architecture of the 1913 German Embassy building. Surveillance, if there were any, was not obvious. He made his way to the Palace Embankment Canal, dark, sluggish and edged with ice.

He didn't see the colonel until the tall figure was suddenly at his elbow, greeting him. He wore a long, belted coat and a fur hat. He affected surprise. 'Ah, Mr Thoroughgood? You are like me – you like to walk?'

So he was under surveillance after all. They were doing a proper job. The colonel had presumably been dropped from a surveillance car when they saw Charles make for the canal. A good place for a quiet talk. 'I do. Especially when I've been sitting all day,' Charles said.

'And you like to explore, to see new places? To meet new people, perhaps?'

'I don't think I shall meet many people here. It's too cold.'

'This is not cold. You do not know Russia.' He laughed and put his arm around Charles's shoulder, squeezing hard. It was a brief enough squeeze to be taken as a gesture of fellowship, but hard enough to be threatening. 'You must come again in winter and go east. That is where cold begins. We can go together.'

They walked on in silence for a few steps. Charles was content to wait. If the colonel had anything to say then he could make the running. Charles expected some sort of recruitment pitch. It would have to be crude and rushed, given the circumstances, and therefore disappointing. He would have expected better of the old KGB. But it would be of a piece with other Russian operations in the new era, blatant and crass. In turning it down he would express disappointment, saying he had expected better. Russians understood irony, or used to.

But the colonel surprised him. 'There is something you have to say to me, Mr Thoroughgood?'

'I don't think so. Unless to thank you for organising the conference.'

'Please, do not thank me. It was happening already. I can make use of it, that is all. You have a phrase, I think – piggy-back? I piggy-back on this conference. Like you.'

There was an outburst of shouting somewhere behind them. They turned to see about a dozen youths scrapping among themselves, possibly in play, perhaps not. It looked like a running fight between two groups. They were a good distance away but their momentum carried them towards Charles and the colonel like a rolling maul in rugby. The colonel turned away, put his hand to the side of his head and spoke into his sleeve.

He turned back to Charles. 'This is bad area. We must go to hotel.' He indicated a footbridge ahead. 'We will keep walking. A car is coming.'

The maul got closer, the shouting louder. It was definitely not play. A couple of youths were being rolled along the road, kicked by the others. Then headlights swung out from a narrow turning ahead of them and a black Mercedes accelerated, stopping beside them with a squeal of tyres. The colonel opened the rear door. 'Please. We go to hotel.'

As they got in, an armoured police lorry, lights flashing, appeared behind the youths. Some ran; others, embroiled in the fight, were still there when the lorry debouched half a dozen helmeted police who immediately laid about them with truncheons. The Mercedes, with just the driver in front, reversed rapidly up the road to the junction. The colonel spoke to the driver in Russian, then turned to Charles.

'You have this problem in London, too, yes? Black boys with knives? Here only white boys but not so often with knives.' They were heading back towards the hotel. 'We can talk another time, yes?'

'Of course.' Charles could make no sense of the colonel's opening remark, to the effect that he expected Charles to want to talk to him. It made sense only if they thought he was volunteering his services, offering to spy. And they would think that only if they had some information or some person suggesting it. He could not think what or who that might be. If, as he anticipated, the colonel suggested they continue their conversation in the hotel bar, he would give him his answer. 'Tell it to the Marines', an English idiom the colonel could add to his stock, along with piggy-backing. But first he would try to glean anything he could about the source of their misinformation.

The colonel did not suggest a drink at the bar when they were dropped off at the hotel. Instead, he simply said, 'We will meet at dinner, Mr Thoroughgood, and talk another time.' He left Charles by the lifts and made for the stairs. Back in his room, Charles pondered the piggy-backing remark. It suggested that the colonel knew they were both at the conference for reasons other than the conference. It was true, of course. But whether it was an assumption or whether it was based on information, inside information, there was no knowing.

CHAPTER FIVE

Dr Julia Andreyev lived in a 1950s block of flats about twenty minutes on the 191 bus from the Astoria. It was roughly the same distance to the laboratory where she worked. To the outside world it was a government research organisation dedicated to assessing and improving commercial products for pain relief. Since it was a government facility no one questioned the need for armed guards, high wire fences and security clearance.

The day she received the letter, weeks previously, Julia went to work as usual, outwardly calm but inwardly in turmoil. Her hand did not shake as she showed her pass to the bored guard at the gate, though it felt as if it did, and all day she experienced the prickling self-consciousness of one who felt she was being watched. There was no reason why she should be, she knew that, but she knew too that she was complicit and she feared discovery. Her heart jumped whenever anyone addressed her unexpectedly and her replies sounded to herself unnaturally loud. Each time she returned from the loo she spent a minute or two checking that everything in her workplace was as she had left it. To everyone else she hoped she seemed normal but the recurring image of that letter, the single sheet listing the hotel charges with pencilled alterations to two of the numbers, made her feel sick.

She felt as guilty as if she had done something, which she hadn't. But she knew she *not* done something, which was as bad. The fact that it was all in the past and that she had since tried to live as if it had never happened would make no difference in the eyes of the authorities. She had lived the quiet, orderly life of a middle-aged professional woman with no entanglements, a few work friends, some family back in Moscow, rarely seen, occasional visits to the ballet, and reading. She read much in the night, mostly history and biography. She was well informed about her country's history and the people who had shaped it. She read widely into European history too, but no one knew that. There had been no one with whom she could discuss such things since Mikhail left, six years before.

He of course was her sin, her crime both of commission and omission. It was not just that she'd had an affair with a married colleague. That was against the rules but not unknown within the department. It could be overlooked. In the words of an English duchess she had read about, so long as you did nothing to frighten the horses you could get away with anything. And she and Mikhail had got away with it, plainly. In the wake of his defection everyone in the lab had been questioned but she no more than anyone else. At the time she was convinced that the authorities either knew about their affair or would soon find out. She had almost volunteered it, hoping that an unprovoked confession would ameliorate her sin. But fortunately her courage failed her and their affair never came to light. Nothing happened to any of the staff except that their kindly and scholarly head of department disappeared and was never spoken of again. When such a crime was discovered, especially if the perpetrator had escaped, everyone knew it was necessary that someone should be punished. Julia kept quiet about her crime of omission.

Her crime of commission was not the affair itself but continuing it after Mikhail told her of his plan that they should defect together. Indeed, she had not only continued the affair but had gone along with his plan to the last minute, almost. Then she had changed her mind. She couldn't bring herself to go through with it, to leave the Motherland – she had never been abroad – her family, her friends, the career she was proud to have achieved, the good opinion of all who knew her. She had nothing against her country, as Mikhail seemed to have; it had treated her well. Of course there were faults, she knew that better than most through her reading, but so there were in other countries. Wherever they lived, whether America or Britain, she would never feel at home and would never speak the language well. True, she had shared Mikhail's unease about the work they were then being told to do but what could she do about it? Whether she asked to be moved to other work, which was permitted under certain circumstances, or whether she ran away with him, would make no difference to the project. They would get someone else to do it, the same poisons would still be developed, the people they were intended to kill would still be killed. She didn't like it but if her actions made no difference, what was the point?

She might have felt differently if, like Mikhail, she had been desperate to escape a miserable marriage. Indeed, she too was desperate for him to escape it. It had been two and a half years since they had fallen into each other's arms. That was how she chose to remember the evening when they were both working late and she, sensing a sadness in him, had made the move. She hooked her hands around his neck and said, smilingly, 'Mikhail, tell me, what is wrong? What is the matter with you? You are not yourself.'

In answer he had put his arms around her and said, 'You, you are the matter.' Then he had kissed her.

But he would not leave his wife. They had been miserable for years, she discovered, and that was the reason he gave for not leaving. His wife was depressive and he believed that if he left her she would be driven deeper into depression, for which he would feel responsible, and therefore guilty. And guilt would poison their relationship. Julia found this difficult to argue with, torn between approving his concern for his wife while feeling she did not deserve it. She had seen her only once when he had brought her to someone's retirement party, a pinched and shrewish-looking little thing clinging tenaciously to the big, broad generous man she had somehow snared long ago. There were no children.

Mikhail had changed when they were tasked to work on the early stages of Konyets, successor to the poison known as Novichok, which meant 'newcomer'. Novichok had been successfully deployed a number of times but had become too well known as a result of some botched operations. It was too identifiable, too easily traceable back to Russia and, given timely medical attention, was even reversible up to a point. The new requirement was for something that left no trace of itself, no tell-tale chemical signature, while being quick-acting and fatal.

'We should not be doing this, Julia,' Mikhail said one evening in her flat, when he had told his wife he had to work late. 'We should be finding ways to improve life, not to remove it. That is what I thought I would do when I became a scientist. I wanted to make a contribution to humanity.'

'But you have done this kind of work before,' she said, 'and never had any problem with it. You have worked on chemical weapons or substances that could be made into weapons. As have we all. We may not like it but we have no choice. And we work on good things, too. Antidotes, you did a lot of work on antidotes.'

'Yes, for ourselves alone. Not for the rest of mankind to use or even know about. It is not moral.'

'That is beyond our control. Science is morally neutral.

Discovery and understanding, finding out about the world, is science. That's what we do. The use that others make of it is what is moral or immoral.'

'That is my point, Julia. We are doing this knowing the use that will be made of it. We are not doing it in order to understand the world. We are doing it because our government wants better ways of killing people it doesn't like.'

'Other countries do it too. We have to protect ourselves.'

'Then we should be working on antidotes.'

'No doubt we shall when Konyets is fully developed. We have to have it in order to learn how to counter it.'

The argument never went away. It would lie dormant for weeks and then something would happen, or someone at work would say something, and the next time they were alone they would waste precious hours arguing. She loved him and soon she began to resent everything about Konyets because it seemed to be getting in the way of their love. This continued even after he managed to get himself moved to other work in another lab. She remained, which was probably just as well because it weakened the public link between them. She remembered being surprised at how cleverly he had extricated himself without anyone guessing his reasons, showing a talent for deceit and manipulation she had taken for granted in the context of his marriage, seeing it as justified and reasonable. Stupidly she had not expected it to feature in other areas of his life. She had cause to reflect upon that later.

Her realisation of how far he had changed came about

gradually, a piecemeal process she now recognised as planned by him rather than naturally evolving. Unlike her, he was one of the public faces of the department and so travelled to conferences and seminars, some of them abroad. He always returned with presents for her. He was good like that, birthdays and their anniversary – deemed the night of their first embrace – were never forgotten. He remembered her favourite perfume – Chanel's Coco Mademoiselle – and her clothing and shoe sizes and colour preferences. He was unfailingly considerate. It was only at the very end, when she was forced to decide, that she realised how deliberate – and deliberated – his considerateness was. After each trip abroad he would have something alluring to say about life in America or Europe. Gradually they developed a fantasy of themselves living in graceful opulence in Switzerland or America, and latterly in England where they played at being a lord and lady on a country estate.

Then, one Saturday afternoon when they were in her bed and his wife was away visiting her mother, he had said quietly, 'Of course, we could make it real if we wanted. It's up to us.'

She laughed. 'We become an English lord and lady? How?'

'Not that, perhaps, but we could go there. We could live there.'

She went along with it, thinking at first it was an extension of their other fantasies. Then, when she realised he was serious, she continued to appear to acquiesce because she thought it would never happen. Until one evening he said,

'We should make arrangements. We should decide on a date.'

'What? Are you serious? We simply resign and move there? We wouldn't be allowed.'

'The law would not prevent us. This is no longer the old Soviet Union.'

'The law might not but the government would, surely. And how would we live? We would have no work.'

'They would give us a pension.'

'The English would give us a pension? How? Why?'

'For helping them understand what we are doing.'

It took a while for her to grasp the full import of what 'helping them understand' meant. It meant telling the secrets of their work; in other words, spying. When he told her he was already doing it, and had been for some time, she was shocked into silence.

'That means you are a traitor,' she said eventually. 'I would be too.'

'Yes, but for the right reasons, good reasons. To save lives and prevent wrongdoing.'

'You think the English would not do wrong, that they would never use what we tell them against Russians, against our own people?'

'I don't think they would. In fact, I am sure of it.'

For weeks afterwards she felt inwardly frozen. She believed she still loved him and certainly took comfort from his protestations of love for her, even though it was a while before she responded to them again. She felt he was serious about loving her, she desperately wanted to believe he was, but it worried her that for many months he must have secretly pursued this other agenda without telling her.

He continued going to overseas meetings. Each time he returned he would tell her he had spoken to 'them' again, that they were very helpful and understanding, that they would help him and her establish a new life for themselves after a period of initial debriefing. 'Where?' she asked. 'This new life – where?'

'In England. Or Australia or Canada or New Zealand or America, wherever we want.'

'I read there are many Ukrainians in Canada, Russian speakers.'

'So there are. It's a big country, second only to us. Friendly people, much to explore. But we would start off in England.'

'I've always thought I would like to see Canada.'

She later discovered that he had taken her noncommittal remark, intended to stall discussion, as an agreement to defect with him. She realised it only when he told her of another forthcoming conference in Toronto. 'This is it,' he said. 'I will fly to London with them from there. You must book leave over the same period and take the train to Helsinki. They will meet you there and fly you to England, where I shall be waiting. It's very easy. So long as you're out of the country by the time people here realise I am not coming back.'

'But I never said – I didn't realise you were really going to—'

'You did, Julia. I told you. You agreed. You wanted us to live in Canada. You said so.'

Their arguments were sickening. Each night she went to bed exhausted, slept poorly and got up still exhausted. What made it worse was that he was so surprised, that he had misread her so completely. He was never angry, never raised his voice, but pleaded, begged and implored. She continued to believe that he was a good man who was doing what he thought was right. But a misguided man. She could not accept that it was right to betray the Konyets formula; it was simply not right to betray their country. Unable to persuade him of that, she raised other objections – her savings, her flat, her family, her promise to a neighbour to have one of the next litter of kittens – all of which he rightly dismissed as resolvable if only she had the will. When it came to parting on that last fractured night, he told her of the secret contact procedure 'they' had suggested: the flyer from the hotel, which would mean there was someone she could trust with a message from him, someone who could arrange for her to join him if she changed her mind. She had nodded tearfully, not expecting to hear from him again.

There followed years of emotional numbness, an ice age of the heart. She worked, read, saw friends, went to the ballet, got up, cooked, ate, went to bed, functioning as an automaton with no outward sign of anything missing. She went through periods of trying not to think about him at all, then would give herself up to waves of intense nostalgia and longing. But all the time she functioned without energy, simply doing what came next, lacking any interest, curiosity or ambition. Meanwhile, in the lab, their work on Konyets was vindicated by successful field trials on prisoners. She and her colleagues were rewarded with medals.

The arrival of the envelope containing the hotel flyer not only filled her with fear and worry but reawakened the emotional turmoil that everything to do with Mikhail always wrought. She opened it unsuspectingly, standing by the kitchen table, about to leave for work. She was still staring at it five minutes later, but sitting now. She did not remember sitting. On the one hand she was desperate to hear news of him, where he was, how he was, that he missed her. On the other hand she never wanted to hear from him again. She wanted the dead leaves of the past to lie as they had fallen, where she could see them without arousing them and scattering them about her, filling her days and dreaming nights. Eventually, fearing she would miss her bus, she had put the flyer back in its envelope and slid it into the narrow gap between the gas stove and the wall. It had made her feel like a criminal.

Which, of course, she was, she reflected as she sat in the bus that morning. Guilty of criminal correspondence with an enemy of the state. Agreeing the secret means of communication and hiding the message were betrayals almost as bad as Mikhail's. If she were caught her only hope of mercy was to plead that she had passed no intelligence, she had done no spying. But would they ever believe her?

Eventually, after a week of dither and restless nights,

she compounded her guilt by twice ringing the number pencilled on the flyer. It was a Finnish number – she recognised the Helsinki code – answered after only two rings by the recorded announcement of a man saying in Russian, 'Room eighteen'. There was no more. Her hand shook as she replaced the receiver and she sat for some minutes feeling sick.

When she took the bus to the hotel on the designated evening she had the same sensation as during those first few days at work after Mikhail had left, the sensation that everyone was watching her. Her neck tingled and it was impossible to convince herself that she looked innocent while feeling so guilty. She stared straight ahead, trying to be what people called stony-faced but fearing she looked like a frightened rabbit.

She had been to the Astoria a number of times for conferences and receptions, but not for some years. The department used it regularly until abruptly switching to the Angleterre. Perhaps the Angleterre had undercut the Astoria or – more likely – favours were quietly negotiated. She walked quickly past reception, still feeling that all eyes were upon her, and joined a man and a woman waiting by the lifts. They were a couple, middle-aged, tall, speaking what she thought was Dutch. They might have been surveillance, of course, but she took some reassurance from them, having read that the Dutch were tall. They didn't get out on her floor, which was a relief. When she did get out she stood reading the room numbers arrowed on the wall until the lift doors closed, then turned in the direction of Rooms 11 to 20. The corridor was clean and quiet, the deep red carpet thick and new-looking, the doors polished dark wood; there were paintings of St Petersburg along the walls. They were winter street scenes, mostly dark and all by the same artist. Not a happy artist, she thought, aware that she was desperate to think of anything to avoid contemplating what she was about to do.

Rooms 18 to 20 were at the end of the corridor around a corner. The window in the wall facing her before she reached the corner gave on to St Isaac's Square, with the magnificent dome of the cathedral to the right, beautifully lit, at once familiar and uplifting. And Russian, so very Russian. She was proud of her country. She loved it.

She turned the corner and stopped. Facing her, her back to the door of Room 18, was a tall young woman with abundant frizzy hair. She held a sheet of A4 paper before her on which was written in Russian, 'Julia, follow me to Room 36'. When Julia stopped, startled, the woman smiled and raised a finger to her lips, then folded the note and slipped past her into the corridor, beckoning her to follow. It took Julia a moment to recover before she turned and followed the woman, who walked quickly back towards the lifts. She wore smart black jeans, Julia couldn't help noticing, tucked into expensive brown calf-length boots. The woman led her past the lifts to the far end of the corridor where a door opened onto stairs. They were bare, stone or concrete. She followed two flights up to the next floor, then all the way back along that corridor and round another corner at the end to Room 36. The woman entered without knocking and stood back, smiling again and holding the door open.

A man appeared in the doorway and held out his hand across the threshold, Russian-fashion. He smiled and nodded. 'Julia, thank you for coming.' He spoke in English, though pronouncing her name with a silent J in the Russian manner.

She shook hands automatically, before she had time to think she shouldn't have, and followed him into the room. He was clean-shaven, his greying hair peppered reddish-brown. He wore a tweed suit, a checked shirt and a woollen tie. His eyes were grey-green, his expression sympathetic. He had something of the manner of a kindly doctor. She heard the door close behind her.

The television was on loudly, showing local news. He pointed to it and, standing close to her, said slowly, 'I am sorry about this. A necessary precaution. I hope you understand?'

It took her a moment. Of course, microphones. In the old days hotel rooms were routinely bugged. Perhaps they still were. She nodded.

'My name is Charles Thoroughgood. Would you like a drink or tea, coffee?'

She shook her head and was about to reply in Russian. 'No, thank you,' she said in careful English.

He indicated the two armchairs. 'Please sit.'

As he sat he moved his closer to hers. The young woman was still in the room, sitting on the edge of the bed, well away from them. The man indicated her and leaned closer to Julia. 'This is Moira. She speaks Russian and can interpret if you find it difficult with the television on.'

Julia nodded. There was still time to stand up and walk out. It was not too late. Except that it was. Just being there was enough. But she wouldn't do anything, she wouldn't tell them anything. She would just listen to the message from Mikhail and then leave. 'You have message from Mikhail?' she asked.

'Not from him but I have news of him.' He paused. 'I am afraid it is bad news, Julia.'

He paused again. He was like a doctor, she thought again as his eyes held hers. And then she knew what the news was.

'Mikhail is dead. We thought he would want you to know that.'

She had sensed it coming but it was still shocking to hear it said. The words were too simple for such a big thing, a whole life gone, disposed of in three short words.

'How?'

'He had a heart attack. It was very quick. He did not suffer.'

She waited for feeling, she felt she was expected to betray feeling, but no feeling came. Then she felt she had to say something. 'Was he happy in England?'

'I think so. He travelled a lot, exploring the country. He enjoyed travelling. But he missed you. He told me that.'

'You knew him?'

'Yes.'

'When did he die?'

'About six weeks ago.'

'Was he – did he live alone?'

'Yes. There was no one else in his life.'

'Was he lonely?'

'I don't know. I don't think so, except that he missed you. You were the only person he mentioned. His life seemed to be well organised.'

She nodded. 'He was always organised.'

They sat in silence for a few moments. 'Are you sure you wouldn't like a drink or a cup of tea?' he asked.

'I will have vodka, please.'

'I will join you.' He nodded to Moira, who opened the drinks cupboard. She asked Julia in Russian whether she wanted anything with it. Julia did not, apart from ice. When they both had their drinks the man said, 'There are two other things I must tell you about Mikhail. The first is that he left a will. He owned his house – we bought it for him – and he had savings from the pension we paid him. He left everything to you.'

She stared. 'To me?'

'Yes. In roubles the value is about thirty million. You are richer than you think, Julia.'

It was an enormous sum. She could not think what she would do with it. Then, like a great ship looming from the fog, came the question as to whether she could accept it. That would be a further crime.

The television was now showing a documentary about hydroelectric power. 'There are difficulties,' he said quietly. She had to strain to listen. The vodka, the first she had had for a long time, tasted sharp. She wondered whether they had laced it with something, then decided it was just cheap vodka.

'The difficulties are how to get it to you without drawing unwelcome attention. And, of course, how you would explain it. That is, if you want it at all. If you don't, it would return to the British government. Or we could give it to a charity or cause of your choice.'

She had to ask him to repeat it, which he did once but then beckoned to Moira, who came and knelt on the floor between them, repeating it again in Russian.

'You may want time to think about it,' he continued. 'There is no hurry. We can give you an easy and safe means of letting us know.' His manner was reassuring but watchful. The young woman interpreted again, needlessly this time. Julia did not know what to say. She wanted time to think, as he had suggested.

'There is something else you should know,' said the man. He paused again, put down his vodka and leaned closer to her, his elbows on his knees. 'Although Mikhail died of a heart attack as I said, we believe he was in fact killed by agents of the Russian state. Your government. Just like Litvinenko and the attempted murder of the Skripals, which I am sure you must know about. And Navalny, your own politician. Only it was not polonium as with Litvinenko or

Novichok as with the Skripals and Navalny. We don't know what it was but we suspect it was the substance called Konyets which Mikhail was working on briefly before he left and which you continued to work on. Perhaps you still are?'

She heard his words, she understood them, but she couldn't react. She didn't know how to react. She did not want to believe she was hearing them. It did not seem real.

'Mikhail told us that Konyets was designed to be administered as a spray and to cause an instant heart attack without leaving any trace of itself in the body. He did not know the formula because it was not fully evolved when he left but he knew that the work in your laboratory was reaching fruition. Is it now complete, do you know? Could it have been that? Could Mikhail have been killed by Konyets?'

Moira, still kneeling between them, translated rapidly and quietly.

'Why must it be Konyets?' Julia said in Russian. 'Why not a heart attack?'

Moira translated. The man nodded. 'That was what we thought. At first. But two autopsies showed none of the damage to blood vessels or tissue normally associated with heart attacks. Nor was there any aneurism in his system. However, there were minute signs of damage to receptors in the nervous system that control the heart. Our scientists say the damage was consistent with damaged caused by other nerve agents used by your government. But those we know about, such as Novichok, leave traces of themselves. There were no traces in Mikhail's body but there was damage consistent with chemical interference.

'There were other factors. As someone who spied for us' – he paused, then continued slowly – 'as Mikhail did, very successfully, he became an enemy of the state. President Putin has authorized the murder of such people, wherever in the world they are. Then, when we investigated his last days to see whether he had had any unusual visitors, we discovered that he had a new window cleaner who claimed to be Polish and who disappeared immediately after Mikhail died. The man used a false identity and we believe he was a Russian spy sent to kill Mikhail. And possibly others.'

Julia listened, taking it in but wanting to absorb it at her own pace, piecemeal, slowly, meticulously, alone. They were expecting her to react and she felt she had to say something. 'Was he not guarded? Did you not protect him?'

'He was not guarded. He could have been, he could have lived in secure premises, but he preferred to live as a normal person with his own life. He had a new name and identity, which was his protection.'

'Someone discovered it?'

'They must have.' He nodded again. 'But that is our problem, something for us to solve. There is another problem, something I want to ask you about.' He took a sip from his vodka. 'I am asking for your help, Julia.'

She waited. His eyes still held hers. 'Mikhail was very worried about Konyets. He thought it would cause great damage to the world, to all mankind, if it ever fell into the wrong hands. Indeed, he believed it was already in the wrong hands because of the use to which your government might put it. He told us all he could about it but, without the formula or without a sample, it was not enough for us to be able to develop an antidote or even to identify it. He said you would be able to get the formula, or perhaps even a sample. My question for you is whether you would be prepared to help us in this.'

She had known what was coming before he said it. She knew too what her answer would be. 'You are asking me to become spy, like Mikhail?'

'Yes. But only for this one thing. Nothing else.'

'If I did, you would ask me for more things.'

'No. Just this. We would never contact you again unless you wanted us to.'

She sipped her vodka twice and looked away from Charles. 'You say you wish to develop an antidote. But what is the point of antidote? Konyets works immediately, like a bullet in the brain. The effect is not delayed, like Novichok. How can you have an antidote to something that works immediately? There is no antidote to a bullet.'

She was right, of course. Charles paused, then continued. 'We ask you, Julia, because we believe Konyets was used to murder Mikhail and might be used to murder other people. Any people, anywhere, whom President Putin dislikes. If you could tell us what it is, how it works without leaving any trace of itself, we might find a way to trace it. Then at least we could tell when people have been murdered, even if we can't prevent it.'

Julia's mouth was dry and she could feel her heart beating. She knew exactly how Konyets worked. She had spent hours on it in the laboratory and so had contributed to the death of Mikhail, the only man she had ever loved. But she had not killed him, she had not done it, she had known nothing about it. She took another sip. It was not her doing, not her fault. But Mikhail was dead.

'You should not feel guilty,' the man said. 'You knew nothing about it, it was not your fault. If they had not used Konyets they would have used something else, once they had found him. They could have shot him, anything. Nothing you could have done would have saved him. But now you have the chance, this one chance, to save others.'

He spoke gently; she could barely hear him against the noise of the television. It was as if he knew her heart, she thought afterwards. She nodded slowly, several times, not trusting herself to speak. Then she surprised herself. 'If I agree, you will give me the money he has left me and if I don't agree, I will not get it.' Her voice sounded harsh to herself.

The man looked surprised. 'No, Julia, the money has nothing to do with this. You will get all his money if you want it regardless of whether you decide to help us now.'

'And . . . I want to know – did he . . . did . . .?' She got no farther before tears overwhelmed her. She bowed her head, sobbing, reaching in her handbag for tissues. Before she found them Moira handed her some, at the same time touching her arm and saying comforting words in Russian. The man remained as he was, elbows on knees, looking at her.

She blew her nose and took some more vodka. 'Did he leave a message for me?'

'I don't think so. We haven't found one. He didn't know he was about to die, of course. Otherwise, I am sure he would have. Also, I am sure he would have wanted us to ask what I am asking now, to give you the chance to continue his work. If you want.'

'Of course I want,' she said, near to tears again. 'How can I not? It is terrible, this thing, it can kill so many, it is so easy. And I do not like what my government does. But I cannot – how can I – I cannot betray my country which has nurtured me, which has given me everything I have, my life, my education, my, my . . .' She shrugged and blew her nose again. 'And Mikhail is dead. I cannot bring him back.'

The man nodded. 'I understand how difficult it is for you, Julia. And so I will ask only that you think about it, that is all. And Mikhail's will, think about that too. You don't have to decide anything now. You have the telephone number in Finland. You can ring and as before you don't have to say who you are, the number is only for you. Just ring and we will contact you and make arrangements again. Similar to tonight's.' He glanced at Moira, who nodded. 'But do please think about it. It is a serious matter and you can make a difference.'

She put her tissues back in her bag and closed it. She felt more collected now, more in possession of herself. 'You can ring me. You know where I am.'

'Yes, but we don't want to draw attention to you. You just have to ring the number in Finland. As I said, you don't need to leave a message or say who you are. Just ring and we'll find a way to contact you.'

He stood and held out his hand. 'I am pleased to have met you, Julia. I hope we will meet again.'

'Yes,' she said, not knowing whether she meant it. She took his hand again, again without thinking. 'Thank you.'

Moira showed her out, whispering in Russian, 'Best go down the stairs.'

CHAPTER SIX

They left the television on after she had gone. Moira looked at him with raised eyebrows. He shrugged, pursed his lips, then cleared away the vodka glasses, washing Julia's particularly thoroughly in the bathroom. When he came out Moira was sitting on the edge of the bed holding the directions paper she had shown to Julia. 'Shall I burn it or will you?' she whispered as he sat next to her.

'Have you any matches?'

'No.'

'Always the simple things that are difficult. We'll take half each, tear it up and flush it down our loos. Don't imagine they're searching our sewers. Yet.'

'What d'you think?'

'I don't think she will. Too big a step, goes against the habits and loyalties of a lifetime. If we had more time and could meet regularly, maybe. But I'd be surprised if she says yes to a wham-bam-thank-you-ma'am approach like this.

She's too innately loyal, needs time to think if she's ever going to change.'

'She was truly shocked when you told her about Beech Tree, you could see it in her face. I wondered whether she believed you but I think she did.'

'She may not when she thinks about it. May suspect it's a put-up job.'

'I'm not sure she believed you about the will, though. Not sure she took it in properly. Or if she did she probably thinks it's a bribe, despite what you said. It's true, is it? He really did leave it all to her?'

'He did. The will was in the house, witnessed by a solicitor. The Office has a copy.'

'I doubt she'd let herself be bribed with it, anyway, even if we could fix it so that she inherits. But it would work with some people.'

'It would. No doubt it has. It's a tactic the KGB tried against us. A pitch along the lines of "Your father spied for us unpaid but we put money aside for him. Now he's dead we owe it to you and your mother. How can we get it to you securely?"'

'But it didn't work?'

'Not that time. It may have done in other cases.'

'But not that one?'

She was looking at him carefully. Perhaps stories had got around about his youthful baptism of fire, when he first joined. He didn't feel like going back over it all now. It would take too long. He smiled. 'Another time, Moira.

Meanwhile, what's the conference drill for tomorrow? More of the same?'

He went to bed that night dissatisfied. Not because the recruitment pitch had failed – he had had his share of failures, as anyone with a full operational career should have. He had thought from the start that this was too long a shot, and had said so. Martin Manners, to his credit, had agreed; but his argument that if it could be done it should be done had weight, there being no other arrows in the quiver. Charles doubted that he would have argued the same in Martin's position – the risk of compromising Julia, whether or not she agreed, was too great – but he didn't blame him for trying.

The source of his dissatisfaction was concern for Julia herself. She had not asked for this. It was not her fault that she worked on Konyets. She had lived her life in a system in which you had little choice but to do as you were told. Opting out without earning a black mark against you took subterfuge and guile, qualities Beech Tree had but which Julia, from what Charles had seen, lacked. And, of course, Beech Tree had opted right out, although his motives were doubtless mixed; he was also opting out of his marriage. What troubled him about Julia was that she herself was so obviously troubled; a fundamentally decent person manoeuvred into a position in which her decency was compromised if she acted and compromised if she didn't. There were no innocent bystanders in espionage.

In the wakeful small hours Charles tried to remember

who had written that one of our most common sins was to use what we should enjoy and enjoy what we should use. St Augustine? Someone like that, someone big on sin, anyway. Presumably the message was that we should not use people but should enjoy – value – them for their own sakes. Spying used people, very obviously; but so did shop-keeping, trading, banking, journalism, virtually all of life's transactional activities. Spying was starker, though: except in the relatively few wholly mercenary cases, you were not offering people a trade, money for information. You were using them as an army uses soldiers, to achieve your ends, not theirs, even where they coincided. They volunteered or allowed themselves to be persuaded for a variety of reasons, good and bad, but ultimately the only end that counted was yours. You just had to hope it was a good one.

You had a duty to be clear about it because you had a duty to be honest, with yourself as with them. That was the paradox that underlay the necessary deceits of spying. It was how Charles had always tried to operate, not always successfully. His unease about Julia was that she was being used without her consent, a one-way transaction in which only one party could benefit and only one suffer.

He tried to think instead about how the conference could last a second full day. His job was done, they had tried and they now had to wait for their answer. The rest, the cover work, would be boring and unproductive. It was hard to believe the Russians wanted a meaningful exchange on anything.

He never found out. He was jerked awake by voices and bright lights. The voices were Russian, rough and commanding, the lights blinding. He could see nothing but bright lights until someone switched on the room lights. There were four men with torches, one either side of his bed, another at the bottom and the fourth standing by the open door. They were all short and stocky, all wearing blue jeans, black trainers and black jerkins. One yanked the duvet off him. Because it had made him hot, as duvets always did, he had nothing on and for a few moments lay naked, sprawling and vulnerable. The one at the end of the bed said something in Russian, pointing at him and then at his clothes.

He knew the form when it came to arrest: slow things down, act weak, frail, more dazed than you really are, answer, comply, don't resist but act slow, slow, create time for yourself, say no more than you have to, make them feel you're no threat. He eased himself off the bed and hobbled across to the armchair where he had put his clothes. He deliberately fumbled his boxer shorts and almost overbalanced when putting them on. The man barked something, his meaning, if not his words, plain. Charles walked unsteadily to the wardrobe and struggled to get his suit trousers on. Then he had to sit on the armchair to pull on his socks. Next he pretended to tremble while buttoning his shirt. It was all designed to relax them, to make them feel effortlessly in charge. 'I am a British diplomat,' he said eventually. 'I demand to contact the British Embassy.'

They took no notice, of course, but that was fine. So far

the game was being played by their rules only but it was important that he should begin to assert his, even though it would have no effect yet. He knelt to tie his shoelaces but was jerked roughly to his feet, a man holding each arm. They marched him out into the corridor where one of the hotel staff, a pale, frightened-looking girl with cropped fair hair, held the lift for them. Forcing his head down and gripping his arms hard, they marched him through the near-empty foyer to a waiting van. It was like the grey police truck he had seen dispersing the youths by the canal but smaller, with no rear windows and no markings. He was bundled into the back, a brightly lit cell with two benches over the wheel arches. Each bench had handcuffs and foot manacles fixed to it. They pushed him onto one and cuffed and manacled him. One man sat next to him and another across. The van moved off. No one spoke.

About ten minutes later it stopped and reversed down a slope. There were voices and the sounds of an electric grille being raised. The rear doors opened and he was taken out, still with a man holding each arm. They were in a large basement area filled with parked vans and cars. Through the lowered metal grille he glimpsed a slope up to street level and roofs on the other side of the road. His escorts led him towards a lift but more slowly this time, as if he needed help to walk. That was a minor victory.

While they waited for the lift he noticed that the man apparently in charge, the one who had done the speaking, carried a mobile phone in each hand. He assumed one was his. Analysing that might puzzle them since he rarely used it and hadn't even bothered to store any numbers; they might assume some sophisticated concealment device and go on looking. Now that he had recovered from the first shock of arrest, he was almost more curious than worried about whatever was coming next, confident that his diplomatic status would guarantee release when the delegation realised he'd disappeared and contacted the British Embassy. Russia, despite regularly cheating in international agreements, bribing international bodies, faking drugs tests for its sportsmen and women and murdering those of its citizens it found inconvenient, was not – or not yet – a rogue state in the class of Iran or North Korea. But it was possible he might be roughed up a little. Not too badly, nothing visible, perhaps just enough rough handling to provoke an indignant diplomatic protest. It would also give Martin Manners a mildly amusing anecdote to spread around the Office and Sarah another example of what happened when her counsel went unheeded. He heard rather than saw the lift arrive because someone behind him slipped a black hood over his head.

Ascent was slow and jerky with no intermediate stops. As he was led out he could see down the shaft beneath the bottom edge of his hood; they were about half a dozen floors up. To the prisoner, he had learned before, every scrap of knowledge they didn't know you knew was a small private victory.

He was led out along a corridor. Still no one spoke. When

they stopped, a door opened and he was turned to his left. He felt a carpet beneath his feet. There was a murmured exchange and then his hood was removed. He was in an office, comfortably furnished in an old-fashioned way. It had a polished wooden desk with part-leather top, behind it a Windsor-style chair with arms and a leather seat and before it a smaller chair, also with arms. There was a thick dark-blue fitted carpet and, along one wall, a half-filled bookcase. On the desk there was a blotting pad, an A4 notepad, a silver pen, a large glass ashtray and a shiny black telephone of an earlier era. The Venetian blinds were closed and the room was lit by a green-shaded Anglepoise desk-lamp. He had expected a cell, but this reminded him of many Whitehall offices when he first joined the Service. Was he meant to feel at home, he wondered? Or were they having a joke?

Except that the unsmiling, grey-uniformed young man who stood behind him, blocking the door, did not look like a joker. He wore a black beret and belt with holster and pistol and stood at what in the British Army was called At Ease, feet apart, hands clasped behind his back. His black boots were well polished and the impression he gave was more military than police.

After standing for a while Charles indicated the visitors' chair and turned to his guard. 'May I sit?' He spoke in English but his meaning was plain.

The guard stared straight ahead.

Charles sat. He was tempted to be cheeky and take the

big chair behind the desk, but thought better of it. He had no idea of the time. There was no sign of light through the Venetian blinds. Sleep, he knew, was the prisoner's friend but time, or knowledge of it, was another friend. It gave structure to suspended existence and captors and captives were equally subject to it.

After what felt like an hour but might have been longer, light began to seep through the blinds. He couldn't see whether his guard wore a watch because the man remained correctly At Ease. He asked to go to the lavatory but the guard ignored him, staring expressionlessly ahead. After a few minutes Charles stood and pointed to his groin. For the first time the guard looked him in the eye, then stepped away from the door, opened it a crack and spoke to another guard standing outside. Then he opened the door fully and beckoned to Charles to follow. As Charles stepped through the door the second guard slipped the hood over his head, but not before he glimpsed a high-ceilinged corridor with a polished wood floor and solid wooden doors opening off at regular intervals. This was no normal detention centre, if it was one at all.

He was led into an echoing toilet and unmasked as he stood at the urinal, the two guards behind him. He was then masked again and led away before he could wash his hands. Back in the office he sat as before, watching the slow brightening of the world beyond the blinds. There was another conversation outside the door. The guard opened it and let in a grey-haired woman in a long green apron. She carried a tray on which there was a mug of what looked like black tea and a plate with two brown biscuits. She placed it on the desk and left without making eye contact. The guard closed the door and stood as before.

It wasn't clear whether it was for him or his supposed interviewer but he decided not to wait. 'Eat when you can, sleep when you can' was a lesson learned in the army. The tea was lukewarm but strong and welcome. He ate the biscuits with no interference from the guard.

He tried to work out what might be happening. Best case was that this was a clumsy and perfunctory attempt to intimidate him into revealing knowledge of Russian case-work from his past. Perfunctory because they would know they couldn't hold him for long or put him under serious pressure. Clumsy because there had been no attempt at cultivation, no attempt to lure him into indiscretion through drugging, charm or blackmail. It was almost insulting to think that they thought he could so easily and abruptly be persuaded to talk.

The worst case was that they had somehow learned of his contact with Julia, possibly even through her. She might have alerted her security people as soon as she got home, or perhaps had already alerted them when she received the letter and they had told her to follow it up, to appear to go along with it. In either case Charles would be shouted at and filmed before being released into a staged media circus, accompanied by predictable outrage that a patriotic Russian woman should have been subjected to bullying and subversion by a former Chief of MI6 who had journeyed to Russia under false pretences to get her to spy against the Motherland.

Yet she had appeared visibly shocked and her reactions had seemed so genuine. Perhaps, therefore, they had learned of the operation in some other way, through a source in London. Just as they had learned where to find Beech Tree. That was the real worst case, the other was merely embarrassing. And, like most real worst cases, it was the one any institution would find the most difficult to contemplate.

All this, of course, assumed that they knew of his contact with Julia. They might not and it was possible they were simply indulging in a bit of bloody-minded harassment. They had form in that.

His tea was long finished and he was thinking of requesting another visit to the loo, as much for the sake of variety as bladder pressure, when his guard stepped smartly aside. The door opened and Colonel Sorokin strode in, still in his grey suit and carrying a laptop. His lined face betrayed no recognition. He took the chair on the other side of the desk, opened the laptop, glanced at the guard and nodded at the door. The guard left. The colonel waited until the door was closed, then tapped on his keyboard. He still had not acknowledged Charles. Charles wondered whether his pendulous ears would wobble as he typed.

After about a minute Sorokin looked up across the raised lid of his laptop. 'You have betrayed my trust, Mr Thoroughgood. You have betrayed my government's hospitality. You have also destroyed the negotiations between us. There will be no cooperation against terrorism. We are suspending the talks today. Your delegation – the rest of them – will return home. Whether you will be allowed to join them depends on how you cooperate now.' His English seemed more fluent than the day before, his tone flat and hard. It was perhaps a rehearsed speech.

Charles felt his heart quicken, despite his confidence that he would not be held long or seriously mistreated. 'In seizing me and holding me here, you have contravened the Vienna Convention. I demand to be allowed to contact the British Embassy.'

'You came to spy on us. You came under false pretences. Your diplomatic status is no longer valid.'

'My status is valid until I leave Russia. I demand to be released.'

'You are in no position to demand anything, Mr Thoroughgood.'

'On the contrary. You have no right to hold me.'

Charles had adopted what he hoped was the same flat, hard tone. The colonel looked down at his keyboard, typed again and looked up.

'You tried to blackmail a loyal Russian citizen to spy for MI6. You used lies and pressure to persuade her. You failed.'

Perhaps Julia had reported, after all. Unless they had somehow got on to her. Maybe they were holding her elsewhere in the building and would confront him with her if he denied their contact, as he would. Not that there was much point in denial, of course, given that they clearly knew about it. But he could at least deny that spying was what they had talked about. It was just possible that they knew he and Julia had met but had only suspicions as to what about, if she was resisting pressure to admit it. In which case he must not let her down.

'I have nothing more to say,' he said. 'I demand to be allowed to contact the British Embassy.'

'Look. Here.' Sorokin turned his laptop to face Charles. It showed him in the hotel room, filmed from one side at about head height, he guessed from the wall-mounted television. Of course they could have concealed cameras in every room if they wanted, to be switched on as desired. The days when hotel rooms were routinely kitted out only for audio bugging were long past. A television was easily adapted to see as well as to be seen, just as telephone receivers used to be easily turned into microphones that were on all the time. But why would they have chosen that room, which was nothing to do with him or the delegation? Was whichever agent Moscow station or the Office used to book it already compromised, or was he or she a double agent? Or did they monitor every room automatically all the time? Surely not possible even with their resources.

He watched himself go to the door to admit Julia, shaking her hand and indicating the armchair for her. Moira closed the door and sat on the edge of the bed. He was talking to Julia, offering drinks, moving his hands more than he realised. There was no sound. Either they'd been unable to remove the television sound without losing what was said, or they had but didn't want him to know how successfully they did it. Either way, it didn't much matter; the evidence was compelling.

Sorokin was writing on a notepad. 'Perhaps you would like to hear as well as see?' he said. He turned the laptop back to himself and tapped the keyboard. The sound of the television filled the room as he turned the screen back to Charles. At the same time he pushed the notepad and pencil across the desk, pointing to it. Pencilled in English and in clumsy capital letters were the words, 'YOUR MOBILE HAS NO MESSAGE FOR ME. WHERE IS IT? DO NOT SPEAK. WE HAVE AUDIO IN THIS ROOM BUT NO VISUAL.'

Charles read it twice, looked at Sorokin and raised his shoulders and hands to show bafflement. But he felt he was beginning to understand, or half understand, what must be going on. The Office had some sort of relationship with Sorokin and he, Charles, was the unconscious go-between. The message must have been concealed in the mobile Martin Manners had insisted he took, which he had left in London. Nothing was yet clear, of course, but looming shapes were emerging from the fog. This was why he had been asked to lead the delegation, why it was such a last-minute scramble with so little preparation, why the delegation existed. It was more than just cover for making contact with Julia, as he had thought; it was also cover for getting a message to Sorokin.

But why had Manners not briefed Charles on it? Need-to-know was all very well but Charles, as the former Chief, could surely be trusted. And he very much needed to know if he was to do the job they wanted. If he had known he would certainly not have left the Office mobile behind and would have passed Sorokin the required message, whatever it was, during their canal walk. There would have been no need for his staged arrest.

He wrote beneath the colonel's message: 'MOBILE THEY GAVE ME IS IN LONDON. THIS ONE MINE. DID NOT KNOW ABOUT MESSAGE. CAN I TAKE ONE BACK FROM YOU?'

He pushed the notepad back. Sorokin read it, nodded at Charles and raised his voice aggressively above the noise of the television. 'You see what I mean, Mr Thoroughgood? We have it recorded. We know everything. I invite you to confess what you were doing. You cannot deny?'

Charles responded in kind, shouting, 'I demand to be allowed to contact the British Embassy.'

Sorokin was writing again. As he pushed the notepad back across the desk he almost bellowed, 'Watch! Keep watching! There is more. Your ambassador will enjoy it when we confront him with this. You think? How will he explain?'

The screen showed Charles and Julia sitting down with drinks. He was talking inaudibly beneath the television, although a lip-reader might make something of it. The colonel's note read, 'I AM IN RADISSON UPPSALA FOR CONFERENCE 24–26 APRIL. TELL MARTIN TO GIVE ME ANSWER THERE.'

'Watch!' he shouted. 'Keep watching!'

Charles read the note and nodded. The colonel let the film run on but Charles was already rehearsing what he would say to Martin Manners. He remembered what Sorokin had said when they walked by the canal, his puzzling question as to whether Charles had anything for him. It made sense now. But if that was the case it made even less sense for Manners not to have briefed him. The only way that could make sense was if Sorokin's relationship with Manners was the other way round, that he was not offering something to Manners but getting something from him. Such as the addresses of defectors. In that case, if Manners was a spy, he would not want Charles to know that messages were being passed but would use him as an unconscious go-between. Which might have worked had he not left his Office phone behind and had Sorokin not assumed that Charles was in on the case.

The film now showed Moira kneeling between Charles and Julia, but he paid no attention, puzzling as to whom he should report his suspicions. The new Chief, perhaps? But he had no way of contacting her without going through the Office, in which case Martin might come to hear of it and smell a rat. MI5 was the natural and proper place but his contacts there had lapsed and he would have to go through the previous director general, whom he had heard was in a bad way undergoing chemotherapy. That left Sonia and Tickeye as the only two he knew and trusted. On the other hand, if he was wrong and Sorokin was after all spying for the Office, he shouldn't be telling anyone anything at all.

Sorokin reached across, swivelled the laptop and switched it off. He rested his elbows on the desk, hands clasped. 'You appreciate that we can now expel your assistant, your woman from the embassy, for activities incompatible with diplomatic status. Unless you confess what you were doing, in which case it is possible she might be allowed to stay.' He had resumed his hard, flat tone.

'There is nothing to confess. I wish to speak to the British Embassy.'

The colonel stood, closed his laptop and left the room. The guard returned and resumed his At Ease position.

Time passed. Charles regretted not having noticed the time on Sorokin's laptop screen. He was still confident that he would be released but anxious, more now than ever, about Julia. There was nothing he could do. Even if he confessed all and did what they wanted, she would be shown no mercy. In fact, revealing any concern for her might only make things worse. Unless, of course, she had been cooperating with them from the start. He almost hoped, for her sake, that she was.

After a while, he indicated that he wanted to go to the loo again. He was hooded and marched to the urinal as before, then returned to the office, this time with a different guard. Perhaps the first one had gone for lunch. If so, that gave some indication of time. He realised he was hungry.

Eventually, after yet more time, another guard entered, beckoned Charles to stand, slipped the hood over his head and led him out.

CHAPTER SEVEN

'And then?'

'Well, they took the hood off when they put me in the car and drove back to the hotel where I was marched through the lobby – attracting maximum attention, of course – and back to my room. They watched me gather my stuff then marched me back down and stood over me while I checked out, then back in the car, driven to the airport, marched through security without stopping and put in my seat on the plane. Literally. They'd already booked me on the flight. Pretty good way to travel, really. Better than the usual airport delays.'

'What about the rest of the delegation?'

'Never saw them. They were sent home on another plane. I ought to get in touch and apologise for causing them to miss any chance for sightseeing.'

'And the embassy girl, Moira?'

'Don't know. We'll hear soon enough if she's going to be expelled. Sorokin was ambiguous about that.'

'Odd that they've made nothing of it. Former Chief of MI6 arrested and deported, you'd think Moscow would make media hay with that, wouldn't you?'

'Normally, yes, but not with Sorokin's agenda. He wouldn't want to draw attention to it.'

Sarah refilled his glass, but not hers. He had got back in the late evening, after she'd eaten. He had told her the whole story which, if Sorokin had been recruited by MI6, he should not have. But there were so many imponderables and Sarah had probably forgotten more secrets than most people ever knew. He trusted her discretion absolutely; if he was wrong about that, then he was wrong about everything.

'So what are you going to say to Martin Manners to spoil his Monday morning?' she asked. 'Nothing like starting the week with a bang.'

'I won't wait till then. I'll ring him tomorrow, drag him into the office on a weekend for once.' It was Friday evening. He suspected that Manners had never been one for out-of-hours work.

'What about Sonia and Tickeye?'

'I thought about telling them first but I don't see there's anything they can usefully add until I've seen how Manners reacts.'

'Ring him now.'

'Bit late, isn't it? Twenty to midnight.'

'Well, he set you up, one way or another. He ought to want to know what happened. And plenty of lawyers will still be in their offices in City law firms. They are in mine,

I know. Unlike the civil service. Won't do him any harm, will it?' She finished her wine, her eyes smiling. 'I won't listen, I promise. Then come to bed and tell me about it.'

Charles was also smiling as he picked up the phone. The Office switchboard answered promptly and he asked to be put through to Martin Manners at home.

'Mobile or landline?'

That was a change. 'Landline, please.' They were less susceptible to interception.

'I'll try his weekend home first, shall I?'

There was laughter and loud voices in the background when Manners answered. 'Charles – Charles, hello. All well? Didn't expect to hear from you so soon—'

'Back in London now. I got an answer but not the one we wanted. Then I was arrested. We need to speak.'

'Arrested, were you? My God, yes, right. But you're okay now, all well, all in one piece, obviously? Good, good.' He sounded neither very surprised nor very concerned. 'Sorry about the noise here. Dinner party just breaking up. Can we speak Monday first thing?'

'Tomorrow. What time can you get in?'

'Well, I . . . bit difficult, house guests for the weekend. Any chance you could come out here?'

'Where?'

'Buckinghamshire, Hambleden, between Marlow and Henley. Only if you're sure it can't wait. I mean, everything's okay, is it? You weren't mistreated, delegation's back, job done?'

'Give me your address and I'll be there at ten.'

He was not displeased to be driving out to Marlow on a Saturday morning. It would give the Bristol a run and afterwards he'd head up the M40 to join Sarah in Swinbrook. She would be there already, getting to grips with the garden, as she put it. Charles was densely ignorant of anything to do with gardens but resigned to his role as weekend labourer. Anyway, there might be time for Cotswold walks and perhaps further tinkering with the Bristol. After he had sorted things out with Manners.

Martin's country retreat was an old schoolhouse, set back above the road and built with a combination of local flint and brick. He answered the door wearing jeans and a thick, neatly pressed lumberjack shirt that had clearly never been near saw or axe.

'Charles, great to see you safely back. On time as always. Retirement hasn't corrupted you yet, obviously. Recovered from your ordeal? We'll go in here away from the masses. Coffee awaits.'

He led the way into a small room set up as a study, overlooking the village on the other side of the road. There were two armchairs with a coffee table between them and a tray with cafetière, oatmeal biscuits, cups and saucers, sugar and milk. Martin closed the door and sat, leaving Charles to take the other chair. He pushed the plunger down. 'Sugar? No, hardly anyone does these days. Help yourself to milk. Bugger.' He had pushed the plunger too fast, causing coffee to well up and spill onto the tray. 'Sorry, too eager to hear what you've got to say.'

Charles suspected he was really anything but. He decided to put his impression to the test. 'Lovely spot.' He nodded at the view. 'How long have you been here?'

'About five years. Bought it when we came back from New York. Just before the last big price leap. Couldn't afford it now.' He laughed. 'But it is beautiful, isn't it? Archetypal English village, often used as a film set. Has a shop, church, doctor's surgery, good pub, used to have a garage and butcher, closed now but they make them look open when they're filming. The props people, that is. Remarkable how they can disguise a place. Sometimes think we could learn a thing or two.' He laughed again.

'I was brought up near here. Frieth, up the hill, on the edge of the valley.'

Manners was wide-eyed, as if Charles had said something truly startling. 'Were you? Were you really? Extraordinary. I never knew that.'

Voices and laughter, male and female, came from elsewhere in the house.

'Wonderful place to grow up,' continued Manners. 'They're all in the kitchen, the others. Late breakfast. Friends we met in Hong Kong years ago. He was in shipping then, very helpful to us. The Office, I mean. They're both fully conscious. Now in Bermuda, in re-insurance. Good thing to be in. No harm in your meeting them if you want. Sometimes wonder about re-insurance myself when I retire. You've never been tempted?'

Charles felt he had his answer. 'Tell me about Colonel Sorokin.'

Manners swallowed some coffee slowly, nodding as he replaced his cup. 'You met, I assume? He was part of the Russian delegation?'

'Have you recruited him?'

'Well, I . . . of course, I can't discuss . . . your vetting has lapsed and even if it hadn't you'd need to be indoctrinated to hear about sensitive casework. But since you've obviously – given your background – in a word, I suppose you could say that, yes.'

'He's a fully recruited conscious agent?'

'Well, I mean, you know, you could put it like that, I suppose, yes. All a bit difficult to say, really, Charles. Goes against the grain to discuss casework with someone not indoctrinated. Sure you understand that.' He swallowed more coffee.

Charles looked at him. If what he said was true there was no need for equivocation. 'Let me tell you what happened.'

He described his encounters with Sorokin and Julia. Twice Manners tried to interrupt but Charles talked over him, changing his story in only one respect, from pride. When he finished there was a pause before Manners said, 'So you left the Office phone behind deliberately?'

'Yes,' lied Charles. 'I anticipated that they would get hold of it somehow and search it and didn't want to risk them finding anything on it that shouldn't have been there, left over from earlier deployments I knew nothing about.'

Manners poured more coffee for himself. 'Never much of a one for the tech stuff, were you? That phone was as clean as a whistle. It had nothing on it but what they – what Sorokin – was meant to find.'

'So why didn't you tell me? If I'd known what was going on I'd have made it easy for him instead of causing him to go through the charade they put me through.'

'Need to know. You know very well how tightly we hold knowledge of Russian agents. You were a messenger, you didn't need to know what the message was nor who it was for. Safer that way.'

'You knew I'd be arrested?'

'Not really, not entirely – I mean, not necessarily. Not the whole caboodle, just detained and separated from your phone for long enough for Sorokin to download what was on it.'

'Who recruited him?'

Manners sat back in his chair, rubbing the sides of his face as if to wake himself up. 'Well, it's . . . you know how these things happen. Not always easy to . . . but yes, I suppose I did. In a way. Yes.'

'You did, did you? Quite an achievement.' Charles looked steadily at him while reaching in his jacket pocket for the office mobile. Recruiting a Russian agent, a serving official, an intelligence officer, was a significant achievement even long after the Cold War. According to Sonia, Martin Manners had never been one of the Office's star recruiters, of Russians or anyone else. He had some operational successes to his name, achieved by getting on well with liaison services during his postings and mounting joint operations, usually technical or bugging operations against third-country targets. They were useful, when they worked, but they were a long way from recruiting hard targets. He couldn't imagine Martin getting alongside a man like Sorokin and persuading him to spy. Unless Sorokin had been a walk-in, a volunteer, and Martin happened to be the officer at the right time and place to accept his offer. That wouldn't constitute a recruitment, though it wasn't unknown for officers to claim it as one. He could easily imagine Martin doing so.

Without taking his eyes off Martin's, Charles balanced the Office mobile upright on the coffee table between them, leaving the tip of his forefinger on it.

'You'd better have your phone back.' Martin stared at it. 'Don't worry, I didn't download the message.'

Martin looked up briefly and half smiled. Charles took his finger off the phone and sat back. Martin reached forward and put it in the pocket of his lumberjack shirt.

'When did you recruit him?' Charles asked. 'And where?'

Manners shook his head. 'Sorry, that would be giving too much away. Let's just say it involved another agent. I can't say any more without indoctrinating you into the case.'

Indoctrination into sensitive cases was a formal process, as Charles well knew. But he also knew it could be used as a blocking mechanism for less acceptable reasons than case security. 'What was the message I was supposed to deliver? You can tell me that, surely. Sorokin would have if we weren't being recorded.'

Martin sighed. 'Okay, since you know about it and you know about him, I'll give you the essence of it. But not the detail. Essentially, he wants out. With his girlfriend, just like Beech Tree.'

'Despite the fact that he must know what's happened to Beech Tree?' He paused. 'And now Grayling?'

Martin looked up sharply. 'How do you know about Grayling?'

'Need to know.' Charles smiled. 'Why would Sorokin risk the same fate himself? He'd know they were identifying our defectors and that he'd be a prime target for being bumped off, so why on earth volunteer for it?'

Martin held up his hands as if in surrender. 'All right, okay. I shouldn't be telling you this but since we've got this far. The reason Sorokin feels safe to come over is that the price he pays for resettling in the West is to tell us how they're identifying our defectors. In other words, to tell us whoever in the Office is spying for them if it's a human source – humint – or how they're reading our comms or bugging us or whatever if it's technical – techint. That's the price he pays.'

He sat back, smiling now.

As well he might, thought Charles. Intelligence like that would be a pearl of price. All credit to Martin Manners, if true. 'But the formula, the formula for Konyets that we hoped to get from Julia?' he continued. Julia had been conspicuous by her absence in the conversation. Manners had shown no curiosity about Charles's conversation with her or what her likely fate was. Yet she and the formula were ostensibly the reason he had been sent to Russia. Konyets was also a pearl of price. Or should be. 'Don't we want that too?'

'Of course we do, of course. But not from Sorokin. Not his parish. He wouldn't have access to it and he couldn't ask about it without arousing suspicion. Very tightly held, highly compartmentalised, knowledge of that sort of thing.' He sounded as if he thought he was telling Charles something he didn't know. 'Really very. You wouldn't believe how tightly they hold it.'

'Is there any way you could get Sorokin to mitigate whatever might happen to her as a result of our meeting? She doesn't deserve to suffer for it. She was loyal, she didn't give anything away, as they would know if they can separate our conversation from the TV background noise.'

'But she responded to our overture. That's enough to damn her.'

That was true. 'Sorokin has a code-name, presumably?'

'Of course, yes, but I shouldn't tell you as you're not indoctrinated.'

'Isn't it better we use that than his real name? Safer? Bad habit, using agent's names.'

'Better we don't mention him at all.'

'So how do you propose to get him and his girlfriend out? He must be expecting to be told the plan when he's in Uppsala. Will you see him there?'

'I'll – we'll make contact with him in Sweden, certainly, yes. Also, he needs to sign the terms: lifelong resettlement here or in the States in return for a full debriefing of everything he knows, starting with the source of our defector details and who's been killing them.' He tapped the phone in his pocket. 'It's part of the message on this phone, which thanks to you he never got.'

'You'll see him yourself, presumably?'

'Have to, I guess. Hardly anyone else knows about the case. The indoctrination list is so small there's virtually no one else who could. One more now, with you. Our Stockholm station doesn't know about it. Of course, we could task them with getting a message to him without their knowing to whom or what, but that has its drawbacks, as you've demonstrated.' He looked across to the tiled rooftops of the village below, then back to Charles. 'Unless you'd be prepared to have another go. Consciously this time, so you'd know what you're doing. I – we – could indoctrinate you into the case.' He smiled. 'Give you a few days in Uppsala. Take Sarah if you like. Nice place.'

'But he knows me and I'm well known for what I am. Being seen with me would be the kiss of death.'

'Not if we find a way to put you in contact securely. We do it all the time.'

'What is this conference he's going to?'

'Dunno. We'll find out. But will you do it? It's a pretty big deal, this, Charles. You'd be doing us a real favour. We've got to know how they're killing our defectors.'

'Of course.'

Charles was conscious of sounding more enthusiastic than he felt. There were too many unknowns. How, where, when had Manners recruited Sorokin? Why be so bashful with the code-name, given that Charles knew his real name? And if Sonia, head of security, wasn't indoctrinated and knew nothing of the case, who was? She should have headed the indoctrination list. Was there even a list? Given Martin's evasiveness and equivocations, he decided to appear to go along with whatever he suggested, for the time being anyway. 'Of course I'll go.'

'Good man.' Martin stood. 'Great to have you back in harness.'

Charles stood. 'I guess I'd better come in and look at the file.'

Martin chuckled and slapped him on the shoulder. 'Showing your age again. We don't have files any more. All on screen. But there's no need to come in, anyway. You know the man himself, you don't need all the background guff.'

When Charles was Chief he had decreed that any new case of particular sensitivity, which included Russian cases, should be untraceable on any Office IT system. It should be recorded on paper in a protected file of which there was only one copy, held in a secret registry which did not appear in the on-screen list of departments. Both file and registry could be accessed only by the controlling officer, the case officer, the head of security and the Chief. No longer, it seemed.

Martin walked down the garden path with him. High white clouds scudded across the sky and two red kites circled over Pheasant's Hill on the other side of the Hambleden Valley. The lawn needed cutting. Charles had one more try. 'I may as well know the code-name now I'm to be indoctrinated. It feels physically awkward talking about him in his real name.'

'Old habits, eh? Well, let's . . . okay, it's Badger.'

'Badger? Isn't there already a Badger, or wasn't there, years ago? An Iranian physicist?'

Martin shook his head. 'No idea. Maybe lapsed. You know how these code-names come round, must be a computer list somewhere that allocates them. God, look at those red kites. Wonderful to see them. They were introduced years ago from South Wales, apparently.'

'By Paul Getty, on his estate up the valley.'

'Of course, yes, I think I knew that.' Martin stopped at the gate and nodded at Charles's car parked off the road below. 'Still got the old Bristol, then? The most distinctive chiefly car ever. Wonder you got away with it. Stopped making them now, haven't they? Or did I read they'd started up again?'

The fate of the late Bristol Car Company occupied a couple of minutes more. Then, as Charles was going down the steps, Martin said, 'In touch with anyone else still serving, are you?'

'One or two.'

'Ever hear from Sonia? You were great mates.'

'We were, yes. She's well, so far as I know.'

'That's how you knew about Grayling, is it?'

Charles smiled. 'Not from her, no. Believe it or not.'

Martin smiled. 'I'll give you a shout when we're ready to go.'

CHAPTER EIGHT

It was cramped inside Tickeye's narrow boat. Tickeye, Sonia and Charles sat on cushioned benches either side of a fold-away table. Everything was immaculate, the polished wooden fittings reflecting the glow from lamps whose red shades matched the curtains. A small stove crackled in the corner. It was four days after Charles's call on Martin Manners and the weather had turned wet and blustery.

'More often than you'd think,' said Tickeye, nodding at the stove. 'In anything but long hot spells it's cold and damp sitting on the water. Have to keep it going to get rid of the damp whenever I've been away.'

Sonia cradled her coffee mug in both hands. 'Couldn't bear it. I've got to be warm. But it's very snug and you keep it beautifully.'

'Warm enough now, aren't you?'

'Thank you, yes. Except in one respect.'

'What?'

'What we're talking about. Thinking of it makes me cold.'

Charles had told them everything.

'It doesn't make sense,' Sonia continued. 'If Badger is a recruited agent looking for a new life in the West, as Manners claims, in return for which he's willing to tell all including the identity of their source here – then fine, absolutely. Bull's-eye. Full marks to Manners. But there'd be something on screen about him somewhere. There couldn't *not* be. It wouldn't show he's a recruited agent or anything like that but there'd be something more recent than the MI5 record of when he was posted here years ago saying he was a suspected IO – intelligence officer – but nothing proved. The Americans and the rest of the Five Eyes all say the same. And then there's the problem of the code-name. You're right, Charles – Badger was issued before, to an Iranian scientist, now dead. It's never been issued since.'

'How dead?' asked Tickeye. 'I mean, how?'

'Pretty definitely, I'm afraid. Executed by his own people. Turns out he was spying for the Israelis as well as for us and overdid it. Made enemies at work, spent too freely.'

'But we change code-names now and again,' said Charles. 'This may be a reissued one and Martin may simply not have logged it yet.'

Sonia ran her hands through her short hair, shaking her head. 'I spent virtually all day yesterday searching every conceivable place on our systems where you might hide a delicate case, and it's not there. I found others – one or two Russians I already knew about and a few dead cases I didn't, nothing very significant and not as many as there should be – but Colonel Sorokin simply isn't there, apart from the old MI5 record. And remember – as head of security I have access to all our systems, just as Martin does. In fact, I probably have more access than him because he doesn't really understand how they all work. Just as you didn't when you were Chief, Charles. Only he's not as bad as you.'

'Progress of some sort, I guess. But if Martin was cultivating a Russian and choosing for whatever reason, good or ill, not to record it formally—'

'Couldn't be a good reason,' said Tickeye. 'He'd want to tell the world about it. Golden Bollocks, remember.'

'But if he suspected a leak, for which there may have been earlier evidence we don't know about, he might have decided to take no chances and keep it to himself.'

'Even so, he'd be crazy not to discuss it with anyone, such as his head of security,' said Sonia. 'What if he went under a bus?'

'Maybe he did with the Chief?'

'I don't think Pamela would have sanctioned an operation like this without discussing it with me. In fact, I'm sure she wouldn't. I could ring her at home and ask, call on her, if you want. She can't have had the baby yet so probably still has some recollection of another world.' Sonia smiled and raised her eyebrows. She had two grown-up children. 'What's more, Manners certainly wouldn't have gone ahead with a cultivation, let alone a recruitment, without tracing Badger when he first came across him. At the very least, he'd want to know if anything was known about the man, whether he'd been approached before, whether he was likely to know anything worth knowing, even whether he was who he said he was. But no one's submitted any traces under his real name or any similar name, or any variant of it, neither with us nor with MI5.'

'You're sure of that? Absolutely sure?'

'Every time a name is entered on any Office system there's a tiny discreet record, recoverable only by a handful of people with my sort of clearance. I can assure you that no one has traced Mr Badger.'

'The alternative,' said Tickeye, 'is that it's the other way round – Badger's recruited Manners. That's where my money is. In which case the last thing Manners would do is draw attention to Badger by tracing him.'

'Equally problematic,' said Sonia. 'Say the Russians have somehow recruited Martin. Or he's volunteered to them, recruited himself. No reason I can think of why he would, nothing in his file – every word of which I've read – to suggest political or ideological disaffection or money problems or personal problems or drink or resentment. Nothing. What comes over is a loyal, middle-of-the-road, generally contented and successful public servant. In fact, more successful than he merits, with a chance of the top job next time round. I looked for evidence of the Golden Bollocks tendency and it's true that he's put question marks over a few of his colleagues' careers while he continues to come up smelling of roses, but there's nothing to indicate deception. A couple of them deserve their question marks anyway. The worst you could say of him from his file is that he's ambitious. But he's hardly alone in that and it's no longer the slur it was. Quite the opposite. We're all told we're supposed to be ambitious, aren't we? It's become a virtue. So why on earth would Martin want to risk all by spying for a bunch of Russian gangsters he's spent most of his career opposing?

'But let's say you're right, Tickeye – he is spying, for reasons unknown. Even then, what he's just done with Charles doesn't make sense.' She pushed her coffee mug into the centre of the table. 'So there he is, sitting at the heart of MI6 and needing to make contact with his case officer, Badger. He wants to get a message to him and get one back. Let's say his message is: "Stop bumping off the defectors whose addresses I've given you because it might bring suspicion on me. Also, get me the formula for Konyets and it will strengthen my claim for the top job. To your great benefit."

'So how would he communicate this? Well, surely he'd use a communications arrangement they'd established. Whatever that is, it would be a great deal more efficient and secure than plucking Charles out of retirement to make contact with Julia to ask her to do something she's already refused to do for the man she loved. Furthermore, to send the message via the unknowing Charles in such a way that Badger either has to contrive time alone with him, which is risky because he has to account for it, or he has to have him arrested, which is quite a big deal. Yet all they had to do to pick up the message was to take Charles's phone off him at immigration and download it while they gave him a going-over. Which is something he would expect anyway, given his background. The Chinese routinely do it. Instead of which, what they actually did was chancy, over-complicated and unlikely to work. Which it didn't. It was crazy, plain crazy. Doesn't make any sense.'

Sonia pulled her mug back to her side of the table, wrapping her hands around it again. 'Then for Badger to reveal to Charles that he and Martin are in clandestine contact and to ask Charles to take back a message proposing a third-country meeting is beyond crazy. Isn't it? If Martin is a Russian spy, they've just killed the goose that lays the golden eggs by revealing it to Charles, whom they know would take a pretty dim view of it. But if it's the other way round and Badger is Martin's spy, then Badger is taking an almost suicidal risk. He doesn't know he can trust Charles but he does know that his own people could grab Charles at any time before he leaves and beat it out of him.' She looked at them both. 'I cannot imagine any possible world in which any of that makes sense. Why would he take such a risk?'

'Maybe Sorokin is desperate to get out,' said Charles.

'There's one world where it does make sense,' said Tickeye. 'The world inside Manners's head. He's screwed up, I told you. Always was. And there's only one way into that world of his. Which is that Charles has to pretend to go along with it, go to Uppsala and find out from Sorokin what's going on. Get it out of him.'

'Badger won't tell us anything he doesn't want to,' said Charles. 'He's a hard nut.'

'There are ways.'

'None that are open to us.'

'I just want to get the bastard who did Grayling in.'

'Which wouldn't have been Badger.'

'But he might know how they're doing it.'

Charles held up his hands. 'I shall go. I've told Martin I shall. But I'd like you two to be in on it. Unofficially, maybe a bit of surveillance, without Manners or anyone else knowing.'

Tickeye nodded; Sonia smiled. 'I suppose the worst that can befall me is that I'm invited to retire early,' she said. 'Which I'm sure they're on the point of doing anyway, as soon as they can find a reason.'

It was another week before Martin Manners rang with the conference details. 'It's organised by Uppsala University's Institute of Russian and Eurasian Studies. Very international, the theme is Climate Change, Pandemics and International Security: Mitigation and Assurance. Squads of officials, academics and pseudo-academics from Russia and China, obviously all themes close to their hearts. Hope our friend manages to keep a straight face.' He chuckled. 'Can you pop in for a chat? Make sure we get the *modus operandi* right this time.'

A few minutes later he rang back. 'Better idea. Why don't we lunch? Most of my lunches these days are such dreary dutiful affairs, sandwiches and fizzy water. Don't often get the chance for a good old gossip. Will the Garrick do?'

The bar at the Garrick was busy. Martin was leaning against it, sporting his club tie and laughing at something a couple of other men were saying. He introduced Charles as his predecessor, thereby promoting himself unless he had been appointed Chief that morning. Charles let it ride. It was clear that everyone knew what Martin did and that any guest of his was assumed to be a colleague.

'There should be a Spies Corner in the dining room reserved for you lot,' one of the men said. 'Where you can plot without anyone eavesdropping.'

Martin was drinking champagne. 'Bubbly, Charles? Always a good pick-me-up after a morning of meetings. God, they're dreary, these meetings. How did you cope?'

Charles would have preferred a beer but wanted to encourage Martin to be expansive. 'Bubbly's good for me.'

'Letting James Bond down a bit, aren't we? Never mind. He'd have been much more particular. Kingsley Amis, who wrote one of the Bond books, always needed a few whiskies to lever himself into lunch. Used to sit and hold forth in that chair over there. Said the worst words he ever heard were, "Shall we go straight in?"' He laughed.

Downstairs they both chose solid club fare, onion soup followed by steak and kidney pudding for Charles, liver and bacon for Martin, washed down with the club claret.

'Regard this as your formal indoctrination into the Badger case,' said Martin. 'Now called Breeder, incidentally. Thought we'd use your indoctrination as reason to change the code-name. S'posed to change them frequently anyway, aren't we? Don't know why Breeder.'

'Perhaps it's appropriate? Legions of offspring?'

'Good point. Must ask.'

'Don't I have to sign an indoctrination form?'

'Electronically, we do it electronically now. That can wait until you're next in the orifice. Much better to talk things over outside it. Frees the mind.' He chuckled. 'Now, Uppsala. You know what the conference is. He's staying with other delegates in the Radisson. We've got you into Grand Hotell Hörnan, which is not grand but very nice, I'm told. And not far from the university area. Took a bit of doing because nearly everywhere's fully booked, but Swedish liaison owed us a favour so they talked to the hotel people. Very good, the Swedes. We do a lot with them, one way and another.' He nodded as if assuring Charles of a surprising fact.

'I thought you didn't want me anywhere near Breeder?'

'You're okay to be in the same town so long as you're not seen with him. You mustn't be seen talking to him.'

'So Swedish liaison are in on the case?'

'No, very much not, they think it's something else entirely. Another reason altogether.'

'What? In case I'm asked.'

'Oh, some . . . some exercise, can't remember exactly, some training exercise you've agreed to help out with. Doesn't matter, no one's going to ask.'

Charles didn't comment on the unlikelihood of a former Chief helping out with training exercises. 'But the hotel will know that Swedish intelligence asked them to make room for a visiting Brit who happens to be, they'll find in ten seconds on Google, the former Chief of MI6?'

'No problem with that, is there? They'll assume it's the usual back-scratching. Probably think you're attending the conference.'

'But I'm not. Or am I?'

'No, no, God, no, don't want you anywhere near it or him. Act as if you're on holiday. Take Sarah. Nice place, Uppsala. Has a river and a castle, cathedral, that sort of thing. Nice atmosphere, lots of cycling, short train ride into Stockholm. Sarah would love it. Just her sort of thing.'

Martin's presumption that he knew what Sarah would like was mildly irritating, though probably accurate. A waiter removed their soup. 'I think we'll need another of these,' Martin told him, tapping the wine bottle. Then he folded his arms and leaned forward, lowering his voice. 'We should discuss means of contact with Breeder and the message you're to pass.'

'Have you been in touch with him since I got back?'

'No, and he wouldn't expect me to be. Too risky without very good reason. But we know he will be expecting contact in Uppsala. We have to make sure it's effective and discreet and tells him what he needs to know. And that he tells us what we need to know, too, of course.'

'Which is?'

'Well.' Martin turned his head from side to side, ostentatiously checking that no one was near despite the fact that no one could have been on his right because they were against the wall. On his left the length of the dining room stretched away, the nearest table at a decent distance. He resumed speaking while still looking at it rather than Charles, as if worried that it might approach them. 'What he needs is reassurance that we'll have him on the terms agreed, including mistress. And he needs a plan, a defection plan.' He raised his hand and smiled at someone on the long middle table.

'Which is?'

'Whatever you agree with him. He'll know best what would suit his routine, his way of life and so on – and when – and you know what's possible and what isn't. You've done exfiltrations before, haven't you?'

Exfiltrations were rare. They demanded meticulous planning involving different sections within Head Office and sometimes the armed services. Fallbacks had to be worked out and worst-case scenarios set out in detail before ministers so that the risks, physical and political, were acknowledged and accepted. Everything Martin said was too relaxed, too vague, too ad hoc. But he had to believe that Charles was going along with it. 'Okay, so that's what he wants from us. What do we want from him?'

The waiter reappeared with their main courses and a second bottle and refilled their glasses, emptying the first.

Martin waited until he'd gone. 'What we want from him is perfectly clear.' He drained half his glass. 'He must agree to be debriefed without limit on everything he knows about Russian intelligence identities and operations. As well as any political stuff he has access to. But the first thing he must do is tell us how they know the identities and where-abouts of our defectors. Which has to be, I reckon, a source within the Office. Human or technical. Could be either, if you think about it. Mustn't forget that.'

That was obvious enough not to need saying. 'So either he gives us a name or a technique or it's no deal?'

'Well, he may not have a name, maybe just a code-name. But if it's human he might be able to describe the source's position, access, how long the case has been running, that sort of thing. Enough for us to get our teeth into. If it's technical, some sort of breach of our codes or systems, he might at least know the area it's in or the kind of work done by whichever part of their technical apparatus is getting it. But if it's human it's possible the Russians themselves may not know his name, as they didn't with Hanssen – you remember, the FBI officer who spied for them, who was even more damaging than Ames, the CIA spy? The Russians had no idea who he was but they knew his stuff was real and the area he worked in.'

'What if he doesn't know, can't even tell us where to start looking?'

'We still accept him. So long as he's prepared to tell us what he does know and help us find him.'

'And then there's Konyets, the murder weapon. We want that, don't we?'

'Very much so, yes. If he can get it.'

'And their agent, the Illegal – whoever it is they've got here – who's doing the knocking off? We want him if he's still here.'

'Him too, yes.'

They ate. Martin's reaction to mention of the Konyets formula seemed almost an afterthought. Charles waited a few mouthfuls, then said, 'When did you last see him?'

'See who?'

'Breeder. You said it was a while since you'd met.' Martin had said nothing of the sort. He had never mentioned a meeting and had been elusive about Breeder's alleged recruitment. Puzzlement and uncertainty washed like water across his features. It was obvious that he thought he hadn't said anything about a meeting, but equally obvious that he couldn't feel completely sure he hadn't. And if he had said anything, what? He picked up his glass, put it down, picked it up again and drained it.

'Yes, it was, you're right, it was a while, quite a while. Necessarily, given where he is. We can only meet in third countries. Usually in Brussels when there's some EU junket, some security liaison thing he can get out for. That's still possible, despite Brexit. I can still get there. Or Vienna on some UN thing – but mainly Brussels. This year, anyway. We had a meeting this year. Ought to remember when but I've spent so much time in Brussels or Vienna or wherever that I can't remember one trip from another. They all sort of merge. Must've been the same for you in your day.'

'They do all merge, in retrospect.' Charles refilled Martin's glass and topped up his own. 'But how long ago was it, roughly? I ought to know in case he refers to it. It would look odd if I didn't know about it. Undermine my credibility.' He pretended to drink.

'Well, let me see.' Martin looked away at the crowded room. 'This year, as I said. Must've been . . . yes, back in the winter. After Christmas, probably. Skiing with the family over Christmas. Remember that.'

'That was when you agreed it, was it?'

'Agreed what?'

'The deal – the identity of their spy and the Konyets formula in return for resettlement.'

'In principle, yes. The modalities had still to be worked out. That's what – that's why I asked you to go, that was the message you were to pass. And then bring back his answer, all hidden on your phone.'

Charles raised his glass. 'Well, here's to better luck in Uppsala.'

Martin raised his glass. 'Here's to it.'

'How's Pamela?'

'Pamela?'

'My successor but one.'

'Pamela, of course, yes. Couldn't think who you were talking about at first. Still getting used to her. She was no sooner in the chair than she was off on maternity leave. Okay, so far as I know. Can't remember when it's due. Used to hear from her every few days but less often now. You know how it is, the longer you're away the more disconnected you become. But I bet she'll be keen to get back and reconnect once the realities of child-minding come upon her.' He laughed.

'It'll do you no harm at all if she comes back to find you've solved the defector problem. You must be in line, aren't you?'

'In line for what?'

'The succession.'

Martin's expression became sombre, almost funereal. 'You mean you think I might be—'

'Why not? You must be a contender, whether you want it or not.'

'Doubt she'd recommend me. I mean, we get on and I haven't cocked anything up – not such that anyone would notice, anyway.' He laughed. 'But I'm not sure she, you know . . . Probably thinks I'm the wrong gender or it should be another outsider or something.'

'It's not up to her under the new system and if you can crack this problem you'd have a very strong case. How could you not? They'd have to consider you, and if you had her recommendation you could be unstoppable.'

'I mean, not that I waste time thinking about this sort of thing, never have, just got on with the job – but if it came to it, Charles, I don't suppose you have any say now, anyone you can talk to?'

Charles hoped his expression mirrored Martin's solemnity. 'Not formally, but I could put a word in here and there.' It was untrue; he was right out of the swim, had no influence with anyone, was not consulted about anything any more. He poured them both more wine and again pretended to drink. 'I still see people over the river.'

Martin nodded. There was something of a spaniel about him, Charles decided. 'Thank you, Charles.'

'Did you know them very well, Beech Tree and Grayling?' Charles sat back, lightening his tone to make it sound like casual gossip.

'Not terribly well, no, but I visited them once or twice. Visited them all, in fact, all our defectors. They have their individual case officers or minders, of course, points of contact at least. But it does them no harm to feel they're in touch with more senior people, that we know about them, care about them. Laying on of hands from on high, as it were. Did you do it when you were Chief?'

'I didn't, no, unless there was a particular reason. Good idea, though. I probably should have.' It felt novel to speak sincerely for once. 'So how many have we left?'

'How many what?'

'Russians. Russian defectors, those whom Breeder's colleagues want to kill.'

'Just a handful, about half a dozen. A couple are very old, not sure they'd bother with them.'

'They probably would, given what they've done so far. You've been to see them all, have you?'

'I have, yes. All of them, every one.'

'And now you've moved them, presumably?'

'Moved?'

'Addresses and identities. In view of the threat. Four down, three to go, so far as the Russians are concerned. You're not leaving them there as sitting ducks?'

'No. I mean, yes, I see what you mean. Though I'm not sure they're all under the same level of threat.' Seeing Charles's expression, he continued rapidly. 'But to answer your question, yes, they're all going to be moved. It's already in hand, I'm sure something's being – I'll look into it first thing tomorrow. But they're all okay, don't worry. We're not too late.'

Charles raised his glass. 'Good luck.'

CHAPTER NINE

But it was too late, too late for Nicky, code-named Kipper. He and Beryl spent all morning gardening at home in Heathfield, Sussex, leaving the house only to buy plant food at the garden centre on the Burwash road. During the afternoon, Beryl walked down to the Co-op to stretch her legs and ease her aching back, intending to buy only some spinach, nothing heavy. But she ran into their neighbour, Diane, who had come by car and offered her a lift back, so she ended up doing a big shop. She and Nicky wouldn't have to shop again that week. That would please Nicky, leaving him to his two passions, gardening and researching his history of the heads of the Russian intelligence services from 1917 to the end of the Cold War.

Nikita had been working on that ever since she first met him. He was always endlessly researching, noting and compiling, but had yet to start writing. She had given up asking when that might be. Soon, he would say, soon, nearly there.

They had met via an online dating site. It had taken a year after her divorce to dip a toe in that water. The idea of dating again after twenty-five years of marriage was daunting enough, but the reality – a succession of men looking for meat rather than mates, keen to talk about themselves but often neglecting to mention that they lived with someone else – made her feel grubby. She was on the point of giving up when she met Nikita: ten years older, gentle in manner, soft-spoken, calling himself Nicky from Belarus, he had shown interest in her, in her life, in what she thought about things. He had taken her seriously. They had got to know each other over a series of pub meals and seaside rambles in Sussex. Only after he had told her of his previous life as an officer in Russian military intelligence, the GRU, did he ask her to marry him. It was not a difficult decision; she was lonely on her own, she liked him, she felt he liked her, and his quiet consideration had earned the approval of Peter and Pauline, her adult children. And she wanted to be married again. It had worked before and it would work again. They were content.

After Diane dropped her off, she struggled with four heavy bags to the front-door step, where she left them. Nicky would bring them in; they were bad for her back. She went through the wooden door by the side of the house to the back garden, where Nicky was lying down at the far end of the lawn. She assumed he was having a nap. He often did that, would lie down whenever he felt like it, just for ten minutes or so, then he'd get up and carry on. One day, she would say, she wouldn't be surprised to find him stretched out on the pavement. But this time there was something different about the way he was lying. He was usually on his back, his forearm across his face, but he looked awkwardly askew this time. She stopped and called out but he did not move. She knew, she said afterwards, just knew as she crossed the lawn that there was something wrong, something not right about the way he was lying.

Heart, said the ambulancewoman, no doubt about it. They tried resuscitation but too late. People always say gardening is good for you, Beryl several times remarked to Diane, but sometimes it isn't. He was such a good man, very considerate, always kind.

When Diane dropped her off that afternoon, neither of them noticed the blue Honda hire car pulling away. It was parked a little farther up the road on the other side, tucked in behind their neighbour Mr Wilson's new white Golf. It would have had a view of the front of Beryl's and Nicky's house and of the two either side. The man in the driving seat seemed to be reading something or looking at his mobile but no one could describe him to the Special Branch officers who made enquiries later. Someone said he wore a flat cap, someone else that he was hatless and had short brown hair. Either description may have been true, of course.

'A bloke, just a bloke,' said Mr Wilson. 'Ordinary sort of bloke. Wore a tie and jacket, darkish, tweed or wool or something.' No one saw him leave the car and no one noticed when he drove away.

When he did drive away, unhurriedly, he turned right at the end of the road, then left at the T junction with the A265. He followed that until it became the A267 to Tunbridge Wells, where he headed for the car park across the road from the station. He parked on the ground floor, backing up against the wall, took a spray can and mask from the black leather briefcase on the passenger seat and put them in the glovebox. Then he took a baseball cap from the briefcase, pulling it well down over his eyes. He got out of the car, opened the boot, put his briefcase down, took off his jacket and tie and placed them neatly in the boot. Then he put on a short blue zip-up jerkin from the boot, locked the car and, as he bent to pick up his briefcase, slipped the keys into the exhaust tailpipe. Happily, he had been able to leave the car exactly where he had found it that morning. Then he crossed the road to the station, fed his return ticket into the barrier and waited on the London platform.

They used Sonia's house at Tring for the next meeting, sitting as before over coffee at her kitchen table. Tickeye, ignoring Sonia's admonitions, discreetly fed bits of biscuit to her dogs.

'So that makes three,' said Sonia, 'with this new Heathfield one. Do they have all the defector addresses? And is that all they have or is there more to come?'

'Manners,' said Tickeye. 'He's telling them. Must be.'

Charles shook his head. 'I don't think it can be. It doesn't make sense, doesn't add up. Nothing adds up.'

'I don't agree,' said Sonia. 'It's not that it doesn't add up but that it does. We just don't know to what.'

'Which is why it doesn't make sense.'

'But it does add up,' said Tickeye with heavy finality. 'It adds up to Manners. He's doing the dirty on us in some way we don't yet know. But we know he's doing it. He must be. It's the only explanation.'

'Meanwhile, there's something—'

'Let me be counsel for the defence of Martin Manners,' said Charles. He paused, realising he'd cut across Sonia.

"You go first,' she said. 'My bit will keep.'

'Sure?'

'Saving the best till last.'

'Martin clearly has a clandestine relationship of some sort with Breeder, as he's now called. He claims to have recruited Breeder and to have done a deal with him. In return for being resettled with his girlfriend in the West, Breeder will identify the MI6 source who is giving the Russians the identities of their defectors over here, whom they are bumping off. He is also to be told he must get us the formula for Konyets now that we've failed to get it ourselves from Julia, which was Martin's first idea. Meanwhile, Martin is keeping the Breeder case and knowledge of the defector deaths very close to his chest until he knows who the MI6 spy is. He's made it very much a personal case and personal mission because he daren't trust anyone, including Sonia. I'm not sure he's even put the absent Chief fully in the picture. So far too plausible. Agreed?'

'You could tell her yourself, couldn't you?' said Tickeye. 'One Chief to another. She'd be bound to listen to you.'

'I don't know her and I don't know how – well, how sound she is on this sort of thing. Whether she'd see things our way or just tell all to Martin and rely on him.' He looked at Sonia.

'I can't help,' she said. 'I met her only twice before she went on leave and I imagine her mind is elsewhere at the moment. I hear it's not been an easy pregnancy.'

'Shouldn't be a bloody pregnancy at all,' said Tickeye. 'Not in her job.'

'And then,' continued Charles, 'he sends me to St Petersburg with a message for Breeder that I don't know about. I bugger that up for him by not taking the phone with the message and he then comes clean – admittedly only when confronted – and asks me to be messenger again in Uppsala, consciously this time. I'm pretty convinced he wants Breeder here, which is the last thing he'd want if the recruitment was the other way round and he was really Breeder's agent. I don't believe he is. Whatever faults you've seen in him, Tickeye, I can't see him helping the Russians bump off our defectors. What for? Why should he? There's no motive. He's not ideological, bitter or resentful and he's not exactly been passed over. Quite the opposite, if anything, promoted beyond his competence – though he doesn't see it like that, of course – and now with the chance of going still farther. I just don't buy it.'

'Blackmail,' said Tickeye. 'They're blackmailing him.'

'Over what?'

Tickeye shrugged.

Sonia shook her head. 'But there is no case called Breeder. No case,' she repeated slowly. 'The code-name has never been issued. The previous one he told you, Badger, was issued as we know but long ago and to someone else. Sorokin, the man he now calls Breeder, the FSB officer you met, clearly has some sort of relationship with Martin which Martin has not disclosed – and I have access to all records, remember – to anyone else in the Service. Sorokin has no social media presence, no contacts from when he served in London, just an MI5 assessment that he's an intelligence officer based on surveillance reports of his behaviour patterns. Which is echoed by the Americans. In short, he's a creature who's been identified but of whom little is known, for or against.

'And now Martin Manners, an officer with no particular recruiting track record, is asking us – you – to believe he has recruited a seasoned Russian intelligence officer without saying how or when. He's even vague about when he last saw him, telling you it was this year in Brussels. Well, I've checked Martin's travel record too. There are some advantages to being a boring security officer.' She smiled over her coffee. 'Martin has not been to Brussels this year. Unless he's done it without telling the Office, which is a serious security breach. Nor has he been to Vienna, the other city he mentioned. Nor, according to Belgian and Austrian liaison services, has Sorokin. Nor is there any record of their meeting when Sorokin served in London. So how and when have they ever met and how could Martin have recruited him? Or he Martin, if it's that way round?'

'Manners was recruited by someone else, somewhere else, and Sorokin's his case officer,' said Tickeye.

'Is that what you were waiting to tell us?' asked Charles.

'I'm coming to that. Meanwhile, our Russian defectors are being bumped off, killed with a poison we can't identify. That's about as serious as it gets, yet somehow Martin neglects to mention Grayling – the second one – when briefing Charles for his trip. Why on earth not? It was another reason to give to Julia when trying to persuade her to help us. Not that she would've, in my opinion. But Martin, who certainly knew about it, said nothing. Why?

'Because one defector murder – Beech Tree – could be bad luck,' said Tickeye. 'Good luck from their point of view. But two is more than coincidence. Two means a leak.'

Sonia looked at Charles. 'Who else could conceivably know? Will the Office have informed anyone? Will any ministers have been briefed?'

'Normally, yes. The foreign secretary, anyway. But we don't even know whether the Chief knows. Judging by the way Manners is keeping everything close to his chest with nothing on screen or paper, I think we can assume not.'

'So back to basics,' said Sonia. 'Who in the Office has access to all our defector names and addresses? Not counting individual case officers or minders, like Tickeye with Grayling, who have access only to the one they look after.

I'll tell you who.' She looked from one to the other. 'The head of resettlement, the head of security, the Chief and Martin. I think we can discount the head of resettlement, who's been in the job about twenty years and nothing like this has ever happened. There's never been any sort of breach under his watch. If he was bent we'd have known about it by now. We can discount the Chief too. She's too new, probably doesn't even know how many defectors we've got, wouldn't know where to find them on the system without someone to show her and anyway has hardly been around since her appointment. I hope we can discount me too – or not, if you think otherwise, but that's up to you. Which leaves Martin. We know he knows where they all are because, as he told Charles, he's made welfare visits to all of them. Unless the Russians got the addresses by some technical means we don't know about, it can only have been via Martin.'

'But if it is him,' said Charles, 'which I don't believe, he would know that leaking defectors' addresses would point to him. So either he wouldn't tell the Russians or he'd tell them only on condition they didn't act on it. And they wouldn't if it meant compromising their agent near the top of MI6. Nor would we if it were the other way round.'

'Maybe that's why they're using Konyets,' said Tickeye. 'Untraceable, makes it look like natural causes, series of accidents. Coincidence after all.'

'They'd know we wouldn't swallow that. Any more than they would.'

'So now that we're all agreed it must be Manners, and equally that it can't be Manners, let me tell you my big thing before we go any farther,' continued Sonia. 'Two things, in fact. Firstly, his slowness in ordering all our defectors to be given new names and rehoused. That's what we did immediately after the Skripals – and it should have been done even more promptly after Beech Tree. I'd emailed Martin and so had the head of resettlement before he went on leave and we both thought it was being done. Turns out it wasn't, not in short order, anyway, though it is now. Martin seems to have forgotten all about it for a while, which is incredible enough. But more incredible is what happened after I heard about Kipper's allegedly accidental death while gardening. I went to see Martin. Barged in on him and shut the door behind me.' She smiled to herself. 'I don't think he's ever liked me, Martin. Always seems uncomfortable and never looks at me when he's talking. He becomes heartier and louder than he normally is.'

'There you are, something to hide,' said Tickeye. 'Always has had. And he thinks you'll find it out.'

'Well, this time he was enormously pleased to see me, of course – great to see you, longing to talk, thank heaven you haven't retired, don't know what we'd do without you, all that sort of thing. I just let him go on until he'd run out of superlatives, then I simply said, "What exactly is your relationship with Sorokin?" There was a long pause when he looked out of the window. Then he said, "As I described it to Charles Thoroughgood. No doubt you've talked to him, have you? You were always quite close, you two. He must have told you about the recruitment." I asked him why nothing about the case was recorded. "Source protection," he said. "In case we have a spy in our midst. I can't risk him seeing it. Or her."

'Then I asked him to describe his recruitment of Sorokin – when, where, how, everything. He said he couldn't yet because there were aspects that were "need to know" but that he'd done a secret write-up just for himself, not circulated to anyone, and that he'd send it to me in due course. I'd be the first to see it, no doubt about it. I said bollocks to that – never heard me swear before, either of you, have you? Neither had he. He looked quite shocked. I told him that as head of security I really did need to know, I needed to know *now*. Then, when he was still looking shocked, I said the recruitment couldn't have been in Brussels, as he'd told Charles, and I asked why he lied about it. Then he went to pieces.'

'What do you mean?' asked Charles.

'Just that. He sort of disintegrated, physically. He looked from side to side, anywhere but at me, and his hands kept moving across his desk as if he was a blind man feeling for something. His mouth kept opening and closing and he was making funny little noises in his throat. I thought he was having a stroke. I stood up to help when he suddenly looked at me – properly, in the eye, first time since I'd walked into the room – and said, "I'd no idea they would continue. I thought they'd stop after Beech Tree."

'I asked what he meant but he didn't say, just kept shaking his head. Then he took out his handkerchief and wiped his eyes. I said, "What's wrong, Martin? Are you all right?" but he just kept shaking his head until eventually he said, "I'll tell you, tell you later. It's not what you think, not what you think." Then he looked at me again and said, "Please, Sonia, leave me alone for now. I'll talk to you later. I'll explain, I promise." So I left him.'

'Any chance he's topped himself?' said Tickeye.

'Not unless he has since.'

'Couple of good slaps and he'd have coughed up.'

'When was this?' asked Charles.

'Yesterday afternoon, last thing. He's in the office today, carrying on as normal. I checked this morning. But last night I wasn't sure whether I should call HR or a doctor or get on to MI5 and ask them to mount an investigation.'

'I hope you did the latter. We want answers before cures.'

'Don't worry, I did. Went to see their head of counter-espionage at home yesterday evening. Lucky they still have one, with all their focus on terrorism. Martin doesn't know anything about it, of course. Nor will he, till they want to interview him. Nor does the Chief.'

Tickeye sat back and raised his hands, palms upward. 'So that's it then, that's us out of the game. Doesn't matter what we think now MI5's involved. They won't want us messing around. Nothing more we can do.'

Charles nodded. It was true. Once MI5 launched a formal investigation they had complete control. At least so far as any official actions were concerned. 'Did you tell them about Sorokin?'

'I had to. It wouldn't have made sense without. And about what happened to you in St Petersburg.'

'Do they know about Uppsala?'

'They know it's supposed to be happening, that you're due to go and meet Sorokin, but not when. They were much more concerned about keeping tabs on Martin, making sure he's not going anywhere. Presumably you won't be going anyway, now it's an investigation and they're in charge.'

Charles shook his head. 'I shall go.' He poured coffee for the others as they looked at him in silence. 'Sorokin's the key, the one person who can tell all and tell us soon. Martin won't talk once this becomes formal and official. He knows how hard it is to get convictions for espionage in this country without a confession and he'll probably get lawyered up straight away. And even if he does agree to say anything, he won't know the whole story because he doesn't know what the Russians intend. Only Sorokin knows that. And we've got to nail it before we have any more dead defectors, whether or not they've been moved. Or maybe dead staff? We've no idea what access the Russians have got or what they're planning.'

'You mean go to Sweden freelance, without telling anyone?' asked Sonia.

Charles nodded.

'Taking a bit of a chance, aren't you?'

Charles nodded.

'I'm on for that,' said Tickeye. 'If you really reckon Sorokin will blow Manners, give away his own agent.'

'Clear him, more like. I just don't see how Martin could be his agent. If he's been recruited as a Russian spy the very last thing he'd do is to send me to meet his case officer, knowing what I know and and in circumstances where we can have a nice quiet chat.'

'All right, but if it's not him, who is it? Who else could it be?' said Sonia.

'That's what we go to find out.'

CHAPTER TEN

Charles lingered to chew the fat with Sonia but Tickeye was anxious to get away. Declining a lift, he jogged to Tring Station, picked up his bike at Leighton Buzzard and cycled back to the canal. Once in his cabin, he drew the curtains, changed his jacket and clean jeans for a dirty pair, put on blue workman's overalls and changed his trainers for a pair of well-scuffed work boots with steel toecaps. From beneath the window seat he took a green ex-army rucksack heavy with tools. He sorted through them, discarding some and adding others from the locker, including a long spirit level. Then he added his sponge bag, shaving kit, clean shirt, socks and underclothes. Next he donned an old tweed flat cap and went up on deck to his bike, where he tied the spirit level to his crossbar and checked the lights. Then he set off along the towpath at a measured pace, every inch the old-fashioned tradesman.

He continued alongside the railway until leaving the canal at Old Linslade Road and heading for the A5. He crossed that and made across country towards Woburn Sands. Light was fading by the time he reached the urban outskirts and he turned on his lights, carefully keeping to cycle lanes and stopping obediently at traffic lights. A couple of other cyclists commented on his ancient Humber, not unkindly. Tickeye grinned and nodded.

It was a route he knew, having cycled it before when he was minder for the defector code-named Ridge. Ridge, an elderly Russian diplomat who as a young man had defected decades before, during the Cold War, was judged no longer to need minding. In later times, when more was known about the Soviet Union, he might not have been accepted by the defector subcommittee. But in his day almost any Soviet official had information worth knowing, whether he realised it or not. Ridge had been a Party official and knew a lot about the Communist Party apparatus within the Ministry of Foreign Affairs. His extensive knowledge of genuine Russian diplomats aided the identification of many who were not genuine but were KGB officers under cover. Subsequently, he showed an unexpected talent for computer programming. The Service paid for training and secured him a career in the rail industry. Timetabling, he would say to Tickeye with a sad smile, became a passion. Following the death of his wife he spent most of his retired days in front of his screen, playing the stock market.

It was dark when Tickeye turned into the road of detached post-war houses, all with spacious front gardens and attached garages. There were no lights in Ridge's and the curtains were undrawn, which perhaps meant he had already been moved. Tickeye hoped he had. It would mean he could hide inside rather than lurk in the garden all night waiting for an assassin who would probably never come. The chances were slight. Firstly, the assassin's controllers might have withdrawn him after the third killing. Secondly, if they hadn't, there was no reason why Ridge should be next. Thirdly, he knew of no reason at all why the assassin should choose that night rather than any other. Nor indeed why he should choose night rather than day.

His private initiative to stake out Ridge's house was born of the feeling that he had to be doing something. It was the only defector address he knew apart from Grayling's and staking it out was the only thing he could think of doing. The alternative – doing nothing – he had never been able to bear, or even contemplate. The urge to act had sometimes led him into error and trouble but he was always prepared to risk it. Churchill, he had heard, had said that mistakes made facing the enemy should always be forgiven. What was good enough for Churchill, he reckoned, was good enough for him.

Anyway, there was something of a rationale behind his decision. So far, the assassin had favoured targets within reach of London. Even Beech Tree, in Wiltshire, was an easy hop down the M4. In the past he had heard of defectors in East Anglia, Wales and Scotland but none had been touched, so far as he knew. Ridge, however, was very much Home Counties. If he had to sit around doing nothing he might as well do it at Ridge's house, where he might be lucky and nail the bastard. Whatever happened with Manners, that could be his contribution. It would have to remain unrecognised, of course, but he accepted that. Charles and Sonia would not thank him for putting them in an awkward legal position, making them culpable, Sonia especially. Charles might be more flexible.

Ridge's was the only unlit house in the road, a good sign if it meant he had already been moved. Not so good if it meant he was already dead. Tickeye cycled past without turning his head, dismounted around the bend out of sight, switched off his lights and walked his bike back down on the pavement. He was clearly visible beneath the street-lamps, of course, but not as a threatening presence. Most neighbours would anyway be at dinner or watching television, or both. He turned confidently into Ridge's drive, heading for the full-height wooden gate beside the garage, reached over it to feel for the bolt and let himself through. Then he propped the bike against the wall, opposite the two plastic dustbins, and crossed the back lawn to the garden shed. It wasn't as dark as he would have liked because of the lights from neighbouring houses, but it would do provided he moved slowly and made no noise.

The shed was unlocked, as he knew it would be. He opened the door carefully – hinges were more likely to creak at night – stepped inside and felt along the rough wood lintel above the door for the round tobacco tin. It opened with a twist and he took out the house keys, replacing the tin on the lintel. These keys were not on the house inventory held by the Office. After the second time Ridge had locked himself out, Tickeye got the Office burglars, the breaking-and-entry section known as Technical Services, to cut an unofficial second spare set. Ridge was a man of habit and Tickeye was confident he would not have changed the hiding place.

As he let himself in through the back door, the alarm began its warning bleeping, but he knew he had time, as long as the combination hadn't been changed. The winking red light guided him to the control panel in the hall. He paused to rehearse the number again, then pressed. The beeping stopped. He stood listening for a few moments but nothing stirred. Then he went quietly upstairs and checked the bedrooms, came back down, closed the downstairs curtains and turned on the hall, dining-room and sitting-room lights. Furnishings were as he remembered and there were signs of recent occupancy. In the kitchen the dishwasher door was open and the machine half full. Everywhere smelled of Ridge's pipe smoke, and the computer in the dining room – which Ridge had made his study – showed a small blue light. Wellington boots and a pair of polished black shoes stood inside the back door on a three-day-old copy of the *Financial Times*. But Ridge's pyjamas, dressing gown and slippers – he was fond of slippers, Tickeye recalled, expensive red leather ones – were missing from the bedroom. In the half-light from the streetlamps the bathroom cabinet looked partially cleared. There was no coat in the wardrobe and no sign of Ridge's laptop, without which he never went anywhere. The move had obviously been recent and quick. That was good. Manners – more likely, people who worked for him – were at last getting on with the job. Too late for Beech Tree, Kipper and Grayling, of course. Grayling's death still smouldered within Tickeye as a personal affront, something to be avenged. At least Ridge would be safe now, his house cleared and sold, and he safely housed in another place under another name.

With luck, the assassin would not yet know of the move. Nor, unless Manners or someone else was informing his masters, would he know that his previous murders were not accepted as deaths from natural causes, despite Konyets being untraceable. If that were known in Moscow they would surely have withdrawn him. He might instead be under pressure to get through his list, to get them all done, before the complacent British realised what was going on.

But the chances of his turning up that night were slight. His earlier jobs had been done in daylight by direct approach, knocking on the door or walking through an open one. He did not go breaking and entering – more likely to leave traces. Nor would he risk needless exposure by calling on a house that looked empty; he wanted a victim who answered the door so they could have sufficient conversation for him to administer his spray. Assuming that was how he did it. It had to be some sort of aerosol for death to be instant and untraceable, with no pinpricks in the skin or tell-tale traces in the blood, no Novichok lingering on door handles. That was why Tickeye had turned on the lights and drawn the curtains, suggesting an ordinary domestic evening. He was prepared to sit it out day and night for the next few days, hoping that Ridge had not told any of his neighbours he was going away or when he'd be back.

He sat at Ridge's desk in the dining-room study, the lights now off in that room but the curtains still drawn, his bag of tools on the floor between his feet. The tool of choice rested on top. Not a cutting tool – he wanted no mess to clear up, no microscopic blood spray – and nor was it large. It had to fit in his pocket, to be quickly deployable and to pack enough disabling punch in the single brief chance he anticipated. If possible he'd do the job by hand, without need for the tool, but you had to be close up and intimate with your victim, something far from guaranteed with this scenario. He sat and waited.

The call came at twenty-one minutes past nine. Not a knock but a brief buzz of the bell, the sort an expected caller might give. Tickeye pocketed the tool and moved swiftly out of the study and through the darkened kitchen to the back door, which opened quietly. Most people waited about twenty seconds before ringing again, which he reckoned was more than he needed to reach the front door via the side alley. He had left the alley door closed but unlatched, so that it swung open silently. But still he paused before rounding the corner to the front of the house. The road was still quiet, the only change being another car parked a little farther up on the other side, an SUV of some sort. That would do nicely, he thought. Very helpful.

The man on the doorstep was raising his hand to the bell button again as Tickeye stepped out from the alley. The man was short and stocky, wearing a knee-length raincoat and an incongruous baseball cap. His right hand was poised above the bell button while his left held a briefcase. Not a chance call from a neighbour, was Tickeye's immediate thought. That was good.

He turned as Tickeye appeared. It was hard to see his expression beneath the baseball cap. 'Can I help?' asked Tickeye.

'I am looking for Mr Schmidt. Are you—?'

The accent was foreign, Russian or Eastern European. 'There's no Mr Schmidt here.'

The man glanced at the door. 'This is number forty-six, yes?'

'Wrong number, my friend. They gave you the wrong number, whoever sent you.'

The man stepped away from the door. 'No one send me. I am sorry.' He turned to go. 'Goodbye.'

'Mind if I have a look in your briefcase?'

The man reacted quickly – he must after all have been trained – but he was slowed by his briefcase. His right shoulder and elbow angled towards Tickeye, his arm bent and about to straighten into a hard chop at Tickeye's throat. But Tickeye stepped back, at the same time taking his hand from his pocket and, with a vicious underarm thrust, throwing the short-handled three-and-a-half-pound iron hammer into the man's abdomen. It caught him low, its impact slightly reduced by the swing of the man's coat as he turned to avoid it. But it was enough. It struck with a muffled thud and he gasped. He was knocked back a step, unbalanced, his upper body bent forward. Tickeye was on him immediately, one hand pulling the back of the head towards him, the other pushing up and twisting it beneath the jaw. Tickeye was not a big man but he was quick and knew the power of leverage. With the head locked firmly in his hands, he went up on his toes and then bent his knees as if to kneel, at the same time dropping his left shoulder and twisting the head further. He felt and heard the crunch and crack of vertebrae. The baseball cap fell to the ground.

The body went limp and collapsed heavily onto the garden path, taking Tickeye with it. For a few seconds he continued to twist, making sure, then let go of head and jaw and felt for the heart. That was satisfactory. He glanced at the road, which remained as quiet as before, then got to his feet and dragged the body by the shoulders into the darkness of the alley. Then he picked up his hammer, the briefcase and the baseball cap and shut the alley door. Still slightly breathless from his exertion, he went back to the study, collected his tool bag, put the hammer into it and knelt beside the briefcase in the hall. It was not locked.

In the central compartment were two books, one a history of railway building in Britain and the other detailing distances and gradients between stations. Both were old and in very good condition, collectors' copies. Presumably they would have been used to distract Ridge, given his enthusiasm for railways, while his assassin took out the small aerosol can from the side compartment as he lowered his briefcase. He would then have levelled the can and squirted, arm outstretched, while stepping back and turning away. There was a mask too but perhaps it wasn't needed for outside deployment. Then he would have dragged the body into the hall and laid it out as if in collapse, perhaps at the bottom of the stairs. Then he would have quietly closed the door and walked away, job done.

Job done now, too, Tickeye reflected. Just a question of disposal, always more ticklish than the killing itself. It was easy to kill someone, much harder to hide the body. He didn't need to hide it, of course. He could just leave it for the Office removers to find. It would never be fully identified, they'd never get beyond whatever alias documents the man carried, and they'd find the secret of Konyets in the aerosol. He'd have done them a big favour.

But the favour would lead directly back to him. It wouldn't take much research to show that he had known Ridge's address from when he used to see him. And the manner of the killing, an unmarked body with a broken neck, might point to someone who had been trained. Not that the Office had ever asked him to kill. They didn't do that except in wartime, Charles had told him. But they might wink at something helpful done on their behalf, without their knowing, especially something overseas. It would be more awkward here, on British soil, in British jurisdiction. Better, therefore, that the dead assassin simply disappeared, never to strike again, presumed withdrawn by his controllers in Moscow. And they too would puzzle over his disappearance, probably concluding he had defected to the British and revealed all.

Tickeye returned to the alley and knelt beside the dark lump, emptying the pockets. He brought the contents into the house, laying them out on the hall floor beside the briefcase. There was some loose change, a clean white hand-kerchief, a clear plastic biro, a mobile phone, a wallet and car keys. But no house keys. Who didn't carry house keys? Only the homeless or someone who didn't need them because he had someone to hide him.

In the wallet was a credit card in a name that looked Polish but no driving licence, passport or tickets. There was a small sheet of perforated lined paper torn from a notepad, blank, and £175 in cash. The mobile phone – which was switched off – appeared to be a cheap pay-as-you-go, but that didn't mean much. Anything could be put inside it and even unmodified it could tell a lot about its owner: where he had been, when, whom he contacted or who contacted him. Tickeye put it down unopened. It was unlikely that its owner would have allowed it to track his movements but it could have been modified by his own people without his knowing. It might also film and locate Tickeye in the act of switching it on. Something better left to Technical Services, or the Tossers as they were affectionately known. Except that he couldn't let them know about it. Not yet, anyway. He put it in the briefcase.

But the keys, the car keys, were the thing, the answer to

disposal. He went upstairs to the darkened front bedroom overlooking the street. Lights were still on in most houses, curtains drawn; a cat crossed someone's lawn. The SUV he had spotted earlier, parked farther up the road, was a VW Tiguan. New, judging by the registration, probably a hire car. He considered waiting until people were in bed, when there would be fewer potential witnesses. On the other hand, vehicle movements late at night were more likely to attract attention. Better go for it now, he thought. Also, if it turned out not to be the right car and he couldn't find another, he'd have to rethink disposal. He went back downstairs, picked up the car keys, put on his cap and quietly let himself out of the front door.

It was the Tiguan. The hazard lights answered the key-fob and the interior lights came on. He started it, unhurriedly fastened the seat belt and drove on up the road in the direction it was facing, turning round out of sight of immediate neighbours. He waited a while, then coasted back down and backed into Ridge's drive, right up against the garage door and side entrance. It was the work of a few minutes to switch off the interior light bulbs, fold the rear seats and heave the body into the back. Although he did it rapidly, it wasn't easy. Dead bodies were dead weights and this one, though not tall, was thickset. Nor was Tickeye as young as he had been. He dragged the shoulders and head up onto the lip of the boot, then got between the thighs, clamped one on each of his hips and pushed it all the way in. Then he covered it with a spare quilt from the cupboard in the bedroom, got his bike from the alley and put it on top. That too was awkward to get in and probably marked the backs of the front seats as he pushed it up against them, but the owners – car-rental company or whoever – would never know that.

All that remained was to ensure he had left no trace of himself in the house, then to collect his tool bag and the assassin's briefcase, which now also contained the contents of his pockets. Finally he turned off the downstairs lights, drew back the curtains and drove off slowly with the Tiguan's interior lights still disabled. The only witness he spotted was the cat, which sat watching on a brick gatepost.

He left town in the direction of the M1, keeping to speed limits and avoiding, so far as he could, traffic cameras. He pulled his cap well down. He crossed the motorway onto the dual carriageway A421, leaving it at the exit to Marston Moretaine and heading through the straggling village to unclassified roads beyond, eventually turning into a narrow lane marked 'No Through Road'. The lane ended at a five-bar farm gate, on which his headlights picked out a prominent notice saying, 'Private – No Fishing'. There was a stile to the side and a footpath notice. There was also an area of flattened grass where cars had turned and parked. Tickeye switched off, got out of the car and stood for a few minutes, his back against the door, while his eyes adjusted to the dark. Army lore was that it took thirty minutes to acquire maximum night-vision but he didn't have that long. A solitary cyclist carrying a tool bag late at night on main roads might attract police attention.

The moon was past full and veiled by cloud but there

was enough light. The gate was locked by a heavy chain and padlock but he didn't bother with them. He took an adjustable spanner from his tool bag, went to the other end of the gate and, after some wrenching, undid the nuts securing the brackets to the gatepost. He lifted it off the brackets and opened it wide, then drove through without lights, stopping to close it behind him. The footpath ran along a track used by tractors which curved away to the left but Tickeye, driving slowly in first gear and with his head out of the window, kept straight on across the grass past another privacy notice. He would leave tell-tale flattened grass, of course, but it wasn't wet and, with luck, would recover before anyone wondered about it, certainly before anything was found. If it ever was. Beyond another wooden notice saying 'Danger, Deep Water' was a sagging two-strand barbed-wire fence, just about supported by rotted posts at drunken angles. He drove over it, flattening it into the grass, and stopped on a gentle slope when his rear wheels were clear of the fence.

About three feet ahead was a sheer drop of ten feet into the still water of a gravel pit. Tickeye took out his tool bag and the briefcase, transferred the money to his own wallet, pushed the credit card into his sock and packed the spray can carefully into his tool bag. He did a quick fingertip search of the briefcase to confirm there were no concealed departments, then put it back in the car. When he tried to take his bike from the back one pedal caught on something and he had to yank it clear, dragging the body forward enough for a foot to hang out of the door and stop it closing. He pushed it back and closed the door quietly. Then he took the car out of gear, released the handbrake, put his shoulder to the rear and pushed. It took more effort than he expected and his feet slipped on the grass. Twice he had to pause to regain breath but when he edged it forward the first few inches the slope took over. The car rolled slowly but when the front wheels went over the edge it thumped down onto its underside. For a moment it seemed stuck but there was just enough residual momentum for it to topple almost gently into the water. It disappeared immediately with hardly any splash. Within thirty seconds even the ripples had ceased. The pit, he knew, was over fifty feet deep.

He pushed his bike back across the grass, pulled the fence up behind him, then rode down the track to the gate, which he reattached to its brackets. He didn't turn on his lights until he was out of the lane.

Avoiding the busy A421, he took a smaller road that ran parallel with it until passing under the M1. By the time he chained his bike to the deck of his houseboat it was well past midnight. He cradled his tool bag in both arms, conscious of the little spray can, and went carefully down the steps into his cabin. Job done, he thought to himself again. Job well done.

CHAPTER ELEVEN

'Can't get over that you were brought up here. Extraordinary. Amazing. Quite amazing.'

Martin Manners squinted at the afternoon sunlight filtered through beech leaves. The leaves were just on the turn; in a week or two the Chilterns would bear great manes of russet and gold. He and Charles were walking through Great Wood, which lined one side of the Hambleden Valley.

To Charles, there was nothing extraordinary about the location of his upbringing; it was no more than the usual result of chance and parental choices made before he was born. It was not even a very great coincidence that Martin should have bought into the area, protected countryside convenient to London, preserve of those who could afford it. But he didn't want to disappoint Martin. He wanted to encourage him to talk. 'Yes, isn't it? I'd no idea you were here.'

'And your sister still lives in the parental home? Across the valley? Little Frieth? Going to call on her?'

'Drop in on my way back.'

'Expecting you, is she?'

'Yes.'

'Cup of tea? Kettle on the boil?'

'Hope so.'

'Maybe cake as well?'

'If I'm lucky.'

'Or toast?'

'More likely cake.'

'More of a toast man myself.'

They were at the top of the hill overlooking the valley, the footpath meandering through glades of tall beeches with little undergrowth. Martin seemed content to meander mentally in the same way, talking without saying anything. His manner was nervous, his bonhomie forced. Charles sought to relax him by agreeing with everything, hoping to encourage him to confide. But eventually – somehow, somewhere – they had to come to the point. He was reminded of another Chilterns conversation with another colleague who had gone wrong. Perhaps walking through wooded hills and green valleys was conducive to confidences. The other one had been a friend and there had been no difficulty in bringing him to the point; all the difficulties came later. With Martin, given how Sonia had described his evident fragility, it would have to be done gently. But it had to be done.

He pointed across a stretch of valley visible through the trees. 'My sister's house is straight across. Up on the other side. You can just see a roof ridge and chimneys. That must be it.'

Martin leaned on his walking stick. 'Fascinating. Absolutely fascinating. Can hardly believe it.' He sounded as if Charles had just pointed out an iceberg floating down the valley. 'Lived there long, has she?'

'Since our mother died.' Charles moved on along the footpath. 'So what exactly d'you want me to say, assuming I can get to him?'

Martin hesitated before following. 'Well, you know, what I said before. An exfiltration plan. We need to know what, when, where and how would suit him. And his girlfriend.'

'We're not putting one to him, then? We don't have a plan? That's the usual thing, isn't it? So far as I remember.'

'Not this time, this is different. Has to fit in with him because of his circumstances. He knows what would work.'

'And nothing else? Don't we want him to identify their source on our defectors and get details of Konyets?'

'Of course, yes, he has to agree to all that.'

'Just agree? Doesn't he have to deliver, before we let him come?'

'Ideally, yes, but if he doesn't already know it and finding out might compromise him, he obviously wouldn't be able to do it in advance. He'd have to grab it and run, as it were.'

'What if they defect, he and his girlfriend, and we get them back here only to find he hasn't got what he promised? It would be too late then. We couldn't send them back, not if they claim asylum.'

'Well, you'll just have to tell him we would. He doesn't know we couldn't. They don't understand our system. If he can't get what we need, he's on the plane home, tell him. He wouldn't like that.' Martin chortled. 'Anyway, look at it this way – would he come if he knew his people had a source who could find out where he is and tell his people so they can bump him off? Course he wouldn't. He'd only come if he could make damn sure that source was silenced. Don't you think?'

'Of course, yes.' Charles was not happy with that. Knowledge of any penetration of the British government was the first question asked of any would-be spy or defector from a hostile intelligence service. It was never something simply left till later. But he swallowed it for the time being. 'And the same applies to the Konyets formula? He can pack that in his sponge bag when he defects?'

'Yes, but one thing you've got to make clear, absolutely clear.' Martin stopped walking, forcing Charles to do the same. 'The killings have to stop. Now. No more. Whether he knows how they're doing it or not – you must tell him from me they have to stop. He has to fix that.'

'What makes you think he can?'

'I'm sure he can, man in his position. Tell him that from me.'

Charles swallowed that too, with an effort. He walked on. 'What do I say when he finds he's dealing with me again rather than you? He's bound to expect you, as his case officer. You're the real deal, I'm just a messenger. What do I say about why couldn't you be there? He's bound to want to know.'

'Easy, he's met you already, knows you're my trusted emissary.' They were going uphill now and Martin was already slightly breathless. 'Might risk drawing attention to him if I went myself, given my position. Tell him that because of my position I couldn't go to Uppsala without declaring it myself to Swedish liaison. Look odd if I didn't. They know me well. Might put two and two together.'

Charles had often made things up on the hoof, often enough to recognise it in others. 'That the only reason?'

'Of course it is, yes, that's enough, isn't it? As DCEO I'm too well known to travel incognito anywhere now. Wherever I go, lots of people have to know about it. Can't afford to draw attention to him, can we? Not someone like him.'

'So what's my ostensible reason for being in Uppsala?'

'D'you need one? You're a private citizen now, you can come and go as you please.'

'But Swedish liaison know me too. Quite well, in fact. They might anyway take an interest in this conference, maybe even in Sorokin personally. They don't trust the Russians. So if they see me hanging around, what d'you want me to say?'

'Well, it's – I mean – it's up to you to choose a cover. Whatever suits.' For a few seconds the only sounds were their feet crunching on twigs and leaves. 'Couldn't it be something to do with Sarah, as I said when we lunched? You could be holidaying with her. Or she could be there on business. She's a lawyer, isn't she? Legal business, then. Yes, legal business. Doesn't have to explain, client confidentiality and all that.' He nodded as if convincing himself. 'Yes, that would do.'

Charles left it at that. Having been summoned to what Martin called a 'briefing to discuss modalities', and having found himself no clearer about Martin's relations with Sorokin than before, he nevertheless resisted the temptation to push him on it. That could be left to the MI5 investigators. Pressure now might provoke some sort of collapse as described by Sonia, and if that happened, the investigation would be expedited and he would be prevented from seeing Sorokin at all. Yet he was convinced that it was only from Sorokin that the full truth would come. Meanwhile, it was important that Martin should feel that he had everything under control, that it was all going ahead as he wanted.

The Grand Hotell Hörnan in Uppsala was neither grand nor large but it was quiet and overlooked the River Fyris. The furnishings were period and the only meal served was breakfast but the bar was open all day, the staff were pleasant, and the rooms, though not large, were clean and adequate. Charles and Sarah had a corner room with a view across the river to the castle and cathedral. The riverside road was thronged with cyclists.

Sarah stood before the window with her arms folded. 'I like this place. We must come again when we've time to explore rather than chase around after errant Russians. When does Tickeye get here?'

'Here already, should be. He's supposed to make contact.' Tickeye had travelled separately. Martin Manners didn't know.

'So the Office is paying for us to come here but we're paying for Tickeye?'

'Martin's paying from his budget, I gather. I'll claim for Tickeye if we have to use him. If it all works.'

'If what all works? I don't understand the "all" that has to work.'

'Neither do I yet.'

'You don't seem very worried.'

Charles shrugged. 'Everything depends on what Sorokin says about his relationship with Martin.'

'You've got to find him first.'

'We know his hotel. Anyway, that's where Tickeye comes in.'

'And Sonia knows about all this, does she? She's in on it, too? What you're planning, Tickeye and so on?'

'She does.'

'Well, that's something, I suppose. Otherwise I'm not sure I trust your attempts to recreate your operational youth.'

'Wasn't my idea I should come. Manners wanted me to.'

'But why? Why not come himself if he recruited the man?'

'If. I don't think he has. I'm not even sure he knows him. But I am sure there's some sort of relationship between them. He wants me to get an exfiltration plan out of him, which is the opposite way round to what it should be. And I'm not convinced he actually wants him to defect. He just wants the killings to stop.'

'And I trust Manners even less after what he let you in for in St Petersburg.'

Sonia had remained in London, helping with the MI5 investigation into him.

'So what now?' continued Sarah. 'We wait here for Tickeye to make contact?'

'No, he can ring or message. He doesn't have to come here.'

'He has a phone, then? I thought he never carried one.'

'He doesn't normally but I bought him a pay-as-you-go one. We can go and find somewhere to eat.'

There were abundant cafés, bars and restaurants, the streets teeming with cyclists and students. 'I like their bikes,' Sarah said. 'Upright and comfortable like in Holland, very sedate.'

They ended up back at the station, the older part of which had been turned into a restaurant. They were led to a table in a quiet area, overlooking the tracks. 'Nice of them,' said Charles.

'Only because we're so obviously the oldest here.'

They ate seafood platters, washed down with organic Bordeaux. 'I assume the Office is paying?' Sarah said. 'We wouldn't normally eat as expensively at home. These are worse than London prices.'

'Better food, though.' He kept checking his mobile but there was nothing from Tickeye. Nor from Sonia.

When they got back to the hotel they found Tickeye nursing a beer at a corner table in the bar. 'Only my second,' he said. 'Thought you might be making a night of it. Off clubbing.'

'They wouldn't let us in,' said Sarah. 'Too old. It's a young persons' town, isn't it? Haven't seen you since – since when? Since you both left? If people ever leave.'

'Since I got my boat.'

Charles ordered a tea for Sarah and a beer for himself. 'Any news?'

Tickeye glanced at the nearby tables and nodded. 'Done it. He's in the Radisson as he told you, with all the other delegates. Reception wasn't handing out names and room numbers so I had to pretend I had some papers for him for the conference tomorrow. They rang him in his room before I could get away and put me on to him. Luckily, he latched on, soon as he realised I was English, so I didn't have to say too much. I said I had the paper from Martin and he said okay, leave it with reception and he'd come down.'

'You never actually met? He didn't see you?'

'No, and they never asked my name. I just left the envelope with details of this place and your mobile numbers. Both of them.' He looked at Sarah. 'That all right? Knowing what your husband is like with phones and whatever.'

'In for a penny, in for a pound. I'm not exactly a well-kept secret.'

'Bit rich coming from you,' Charles said to Tickeye. 'The only phone you've got is that one I gave you. Lent you.'

'Only one I'm admitting to.' Tickeye grinned and reached into the pocket of his jerkin. 'Picked up a conference programme on my way out.'

'Picked up?'

'Bloke left it on his seat when he went to the bar.'

The conference was two full days, mostly presentations in a university lecture hall but including a tour of the castle and museum during the afternoon of the first day. There was a formal dinner in the evening.

'They don't seem to have any free time,' said Charles. 'I'll just have to wait here and see if he calls.'

'While I shop and explore,' said Sarah.

'And I hang around outside whichever building he's in and tail him wherever he goes?' said Tickeye.

'And let me know if he's heading this way. But not just surveillance. Counter-surveillance too. I want to know if anyone else is on his tail. If he's under the slightest suspicion, as he well might be by now, his own people will be watching him.'

'They wouldn't let him out if he was, would they?'

'Depends how much suspicion and whether this is a place where they feel confident about operating. As they well might. Wouldn't be the first time they've lifted one of their own off a foreign street and given him a free ride home in a car boot. Or coffin.'

The next morning passed uneventfully. Tickeye identified Sorokin leaving the Radisson with the other delegates and followed them to the conference centre. Sorokin wore an Austrian Loden coat and chatted in a mixture of Russian and English. Tickeye couldn't get close enough to hear what was said and couldn't get beyond the main entrance hall to the conference centre. He installed himself in a coffee house in the square outside, settled down behind a *New York Times*, and rang Charles.

'Should be okay here all morning, so long as the Office is happy to pay for bloody expensive coffees.'

Charles hadn't told him who was paying. 'According to the programme they've got lunch in the conference centre so you may not see him until the end of the day. Unless he skives off. But I would have thought he wouldn't want to draw attention to himself by skipping sessions. So have a wander if you feel like it.'

'You're hanging around the hotel all day, then?'

'I have to.'

Espionage operations often resembled war: 90 per cent waiting. Charles had lost count of the hotels, borrowed flats with multiple entrances, or safe houses in which he had waited for agents, or prospective agents, around the world. Or sometimes just for phone calls. Many were late, some never came. But even for the punctual you had to be there in advance and leave afterwards, hoping to focus hostile attention on yourself rather than the agent, and draw it away.

Solitude suited him so long as he knew it was temporary. He never felt lonely when alone, not even during days and nights in remote places, under alias and business cover, with no umbilical cord to the Office, no contact with the local MI6 station, no diplomatic cover in the event of arrest, no guarantee that the agent or prospective agent would show up, no knowing he would agree if he did, and no certainty that he wasn't a double agent about to shop him.

But there was the certainty of sympathy and under-standing if he returned without a result, whether or not it was his fault. In a way, that made it worse, reinforcing his sense of failure. During such waits he often reflected on the long-term Illegals whom the Russians and Chinese regularly sent to the West, resilient men and women who spied for decades under deep and elaborate cover. By the time they retired, some had spent more of their lives living abroad as someone else than in their own country as themselves. They had seen the alternatives and didn't always take well to retirement at home. Cleaner Bob, whoever he really was, was probably a short-term deployment, an assassin sent to work his way through the list of defectors. He would be a great catch if only he could be caught, but unless there was forensic evidence linking him with the murders, he would get away with it. Spying was not – or not yet - a crime in Britain and he would be welcomed back to Russia with medals and a good pension. They looked after their own.

Not that waiting and sipping coffee in the Hotell Hörnan was anything like some of those earlier deployments. It was calm and quiet inside, life outside was orderly and Sarah was pleased to have time off to explore a new town. For Charles there was the chance to do what he often complained he never had time for: to read at length. He had downloaded the complete works of Henry James onto his Kindle. Now he would discover whether he really would read at length, or whether he never seemed to have time because he really didn't want it.

But he was not to find out that day. He had just settled at a table with a view of the entrance when his phone buzzed.

'Got you at last. Are you okay to speak? I'm ringing from home,' said Sonia. She sounded urgent. 'Tried to contact you last night. Something wrong with your mobile?'

'No, it was me, not it. I bought this new phone just for this trip and forgot to tell it it's abroad until a while after we got here. It needs to be—'

Sonia sighed theatrically. 'God you're hopeless. Don't get any better, do you? No one would give you a job now. Anyway, I was in the Office yesterday and ran into our friend scooting off early with his travel bag. He was waiting for the lift and obviously didn't want to talk, so naturally I hung around and made him. I said, "What's this, spot of well-earned leave?" He laughed and started to say yes then changed it to, "Well, no, not really, more of an op. But in a nice place, almost like leave."

'I said, "Not going to tell me where that is, are you? I could do with somewhere new and nice to go." He just laughed and then the lift came. So I wandered along the corridor to his office and said to Amanda, whom we are not supposed to call his secretary, "Martin just nabbed me on his way out. He wants a meeting when he's back from – God, where is it? He's only just this minute told me and already I've forgotten."

'"Leave," she said. "He's taking two days' leave. For once. Means I can catch up a bit."

'So I said, "Leave? He didn't confess to that. He just said he was going to – oh, for God's sake, that place . . . you know . . ."'

'"Sweden. I've just booked his flights to Stockholm. All very last minute."

'So I said lucky him, and didn't his wife have Swedish

connections, family or something? Amanda said yes, but Manners was travelling on his own, going fishing with an old friend.

'So there you are,' Sonia concluded. 'Expect him in Uppsala. But why, what on earth's he up to? Have you heard from him?'

'Nothing.'

'Any luck yet?'

'All okay so far. Our friend is definitely here, the message was delivered. I'm waiting now for him to respond. If he does. You don't think he – Martin – has got wind of the investigation do you? Doing a runner?'

'Doubt it. You know how anally retentive they are over the river. With this sort of thing they don't tell anyone anything and grind slowly but very, very small. You don't hear anything for ages and then – wham – there's a great fat file of evidence.'

'Usually with the conclusion that they can't do anything because the law doesn't permit.'

'But what can he be up to? Is he trying to queer your pitch in some way, intercept your friend to make sure he says the right things to you? Or doesn't say the wrong things? If so he's left it pretty late, and why on earth send you to meet him anyway if there's stuff he doesn't want to come out?'

'He's left it too late anyway. He's arriving now.'

'Who – Martin?'

'No, our man. Ring you back.'

The tall figure of Sorokin, hatless, hands in the pockets of his Loden coat, was crossing the road from the river side. He looked unhurried, purposeful and confident. Charles got up and stood in the middle of the lobby where Sorokin was bound to see him. Sorokin came up the steps two at a time; Charles caught his eye and turned towards the single lift. A woman had already pressed the button for it. Charles fell in behind her, aware of Sorokin behind him. The lift could only be used with the room key card, which was why they would have to use it together. Sorokin had grasped that without any signalling. It helped to be dealing with another intelligence officer: they thought as you thought. But that could also be the problem.

They ascended in silence. The woman got out on their floor but fortunately turned right. Charles turned left, with Sorokin following at a distance.

'A nice view,' said Sorokin, looking out over the river after Charles had closed the door behind them. 'Better than mine. But mine is more expensive.'

'How long have you got?' It was the standard opening.

'Twenty minutes. I told my group I have official business.' He smiled. 'They ask no questions.'

They sat. Charles offered coffee. Sorokin shook his head. 'What do you want?' asked Charles.

'Martin has told you, I think?'

'In outline. I want to hear it from you.'

'A British passport and right of permanent residence for me and Svetlana, my what you call partner now. And a house and a pension. But we might not stay in Britain. We might go to America.'

'In return for?'

'In return I will tell you all I know about the Russian intelligence agencies in which I have spent my career, including the FSO, the President's Federal Protection Service, which I work with.'

Charles nodded. 'As Martin will have explained, we must get agreement from the Home Office and the Foreign Office, which can take time. Meanwhile we need down-payment as proof of your access and good intent.'

Sorokin frowned. 'You have agreement already, I think. Martin told me.'

Charles didn't believe that. Martin would surely have mentioned an agreement and anyway there would have been evidence of submissions, costings and comments. It was perhaps just possible to do something in the Office without a paper or screen trail but not something involving other departments. Sonia would certainly have found it. 'When did he tell you that?'

'When we last spoke. He tells me. All is agreed, he says.'

'When was that? And where?'

'He does not tell you?'

Charles didn't want him to suspect there was blue water between him and Martin. At least not yet. 'He dealt with that side of it himself. I haven't had anything to do with it. What about the down-payment?'

'You do not know? He has not told you?'

'I want to hear it from you.'

Sorokin's heavily lined features became impassive, his eyes assessing. He was wary now, no longer quite sure what he was dealing with.

'I want to hear about your source in MI6,' said Charles slowly. 'Your source for the addresses of the defectors you have murdered. Are murdering.'

'Martin has not told you?'

'Martin has discussed it with me but I want to hear it from you. From the horse's mouth, we sometimes say.'

'You do not trust Martin? Your colleague? The Deputy Chief Executive Officer of MI6?'

'Trust but check, that was the motto in my time. Always check.' Charles smiled. 'Meanwhile, congratulations on using the latest titles. You're ahead of me.'

Sorokin stared for a few seconds more, then nodded. 'Very well. The source is Martin. I think he has told you this?'

Charles stared back at the face before him. For a moment it felt as if not only his heart and lungs had stopped, but his brain. He couldn't make sense of it. Confirmation that Martin was a traitor was enough to give pause, but that he should deliberately enable Charles to discover it was inexplicable, a mental brick wall. Eventually, a slither of memory came to his rescue. Something Sonia had said.

'I want to hear exactly how you did it,' he said.

To his relief, Sorokin smiled. 'Our file does not record Charles Thoroughgood as a technical expert. In fact, the opposite. One of your weaknesses.'

Charles silently blessed Sonia. 'Explain in layman's terms.' He remembered now. *Unless the Russians had got the addresses by some technical means we don't know about*, she had said. And that was it. They had left that possibility on the cutting-room floor, unaddressed. 'Briefly. You haven't got much time.'

Sorokin took his mobile from his pocket and waved it in front of Charles. 'It was this. Martin's mobile. We collect the mobile numbers of MI6 headquarters staff. It is easy. We identified Martin's and we followed it, that is all. Which means we followed him. He leaves it on so we can follow it to his house in the country. We can monitor it remotely from our embassy in London. Even from Moscow. We follow him from mast to mast as he travels anywhere in England. He visited places which have no official business, no offices or departments, yet he visits in working hours. Perhaps he has many girlfriends, we thought. That would be nice to know.' Sorokin smiled again. 'And so we check his call history and we find he makes calls to places before and after each visit. We become interested in these numbers and we monitored them live. What we found was not girlfriends – sad for Martin – but our spies. Your defectors. Martin visited them all before Christmas last year, giving presents. He rang them before and afterwards and sometimes they rang him. It was easy to work out their addresses. Then our president ordered us to take action in accordance with Russian law for traitors.'

Charles's stare provoked another smile from Sorokin. 'You English are less clever as you think.'

'How did you get the numbers? How was it so easy?'

'Your staff do not take mobiles into their offices, they have to leave them in cages in the entrance. Except senior people. That is true, yes? Correct procedure for most staff, very good. But when they leave at the end of the day they collect their phones and when they are outside the building, what do they do? They check them. And so at the same time every working day many numbers light up our screens, all around MI6 headquarters. We study them – pattern analysis, you call it – and slowly, number by number, we learn who your staff are, where they live, who their friends are, where they go, what they do. Sometimes their bank details and their little private things they keep secret, even from MI6. Very interesting for us. And very simple. But you must know this technique, your technical people must know it, your GCHQ must do it to others – to us – but you do nothing about it. You must know it is weakness in your system but you let it happen. Your staff lack discipline, Mr Thoroughgood. Perhaps you are afraid of them?'

It was a known problem. Charles remembered it from his time, when he had banned the use of mobiles in Head Office. That had been relatively straightforward but proximity use was an altogether more difficult problem. They had tested it themselves, GCHQ had demonstrated what could be learned. Staff were periodically reminded not to switch on their phones until they were some distance away from Head Office or were merged with people leaving other offices, and for a while it would improve. But Sorokin was right:

they let it happen. The fact that everyone else did too was no excuse. 'Is that how you identified Martin's phone?'

'That might have been difficult, with so many numbers. But you made it easy for us. Not many years ago you relax rules for senior staff. Perhaps not you – perhaps before you are in charge, yes? They can have their phones with them all the time, even at their desks, just the big pigs, not the little pigs. We were very pleased about that. We made good progress with many but suddenly, later, it stopped. That is when you are the Chief, yes? You became biggest pig and it stops. But after you it starts again. Martin is promoted and becomes big pig and uses his mobile at work more than anyone and so we concentrate on him. We learn everything about him, who he sees, where he goes. No girlfriend, I'm afraid. Sad for him.'

'Sad for the defectors, too.'

Sorokin shrugged. 'They took their chances. They knew the penalty.'

'But you now want to do the same?'

'It will be different. You know your weakness. You will do something to improve it.'

What he said was true. When Charles was brought back from early retirement and unexpectedly made Chief, years before, he had been surprised to find that senior staff were permitted to keep their phones at their desks. The reasons given were those that Martin had given recently – that in the modern world people without mobiles were not taken seriously, were not plausible interlocutors for movers and shakers in Whitehall and beyond, MI6 had to move with the times. Then he learned that the phones had been provided free by a telecommunications company contracted by the Office, as again now, according to Martin. This was presented as an additional reason for having them. When he asked about Chinese-made components, what they might be capable of if tweaked by their manufacturers, no one could tell him. He had accordingly changed the rules on the third day of his tenure. It was not popular with his senior staff, though he had heard that it played well with their juniors. His ruling was reversed.

'When did you tell Martin how you were doing it?'

'About a month ago. Before he sent you to St Petersburg.'

'Where?'

'Where? What do you mean, where?'

'Where did you tell him? Where did you meet?'

Sorokin looked puzzled. 'He didn't tell you?'

'I want to hear it from you. I want your side of it.'

'We did not meet. Of course we did not. We have never met. You must know that, I think? I called him at his home. On his mobile. I told him who I was and thanked him for helping us to identify our traitors living in England. He was very surprised. He did not believe. Then I told him their addresses. He was quite upset, I think. I also told him he is responsible for their deaths. This would be bad for him and for the MI6 if it was known. Very bad for him, the end of his career. However, I could stop the assassination programme and withdraw our excellent agent if he arranged for me and Svetlana to become defectors. And no one would ever know.'

'He agreed?'

Sorokin shook his head, smiling. 'Not at first. He said it was not possible. I told him I would call again in twenty-four hours and if he did not agree, our programme would continue and when we had finished, the world would know because we would tell them. After twenty-four hours I call again and he agrees. He said he would have to do it very secretly and that he would send a visitor to Russia with a mobile on which the arrangements would be stored. He did not say the visitor would be you but he said the visitor would not know the message. All I must do was download what was in his mobile and give it back. But when I saw that the messenger was you I thought you must know about it even if you did not know what the message said. And then, of course, you bring another mobile, wrong mobile. Deliberately, Martin tells me, because you did not trust MI6 phone. You were right but for wrong reasons.'

Charles said nothing. So Martin was not a Russian spy, just an ambitious and deceitful officer struggling to save his career. Foolishly, because owning up would have been to his credit, would have earned him respectful retirement with reputation and honour – possibly with the addition of a CMG – intact. Nor was Sorokin a British spy, not really. He was an intelligence officer seeking a change of life, willing to trade, a one-off deal. It had been done before, as he well knew. But Martin was doubly foolish; a defection demanded a bureaucratic process, a permanent financial commitment, it was not something that could be fixed on the sly. Others would have to know about it and agree it. He knew that and must surely have realised he was running into the buffers. That might explain his breakdown when challenged by Sonia, but it didn't explain why he was on his way to Sweden now.

The silence continued but Charles knew he had to end it soon. If he allowed Sorokin to see how little he had known about this he would lose whatever respect Sorokin might have for him. He would no longer be authoritative, no longer be seen as one who could influence Sorokin's future, merely an ill-informed messenger struggling to keep up with the story, a pawn rather than a prince bishop, a mere Rosencrantz or Guildenstern.

'The reason I wanted to hear it from you as well as from Martin is that I wanted a full picture of what was actually said.' He spoke slowly, as if after long consideration. 'You see, what worries me about your conversations with Martin is that your own people might have monitored them without your knowledge. It may not be only your screen that lights up when Martin's mobile is active.'

'Of course I have thought about that. I ring only from a mobile no one knows about and only when I am abroad, usually from Finland where I go frequently. They would pick up the calling number and the approximate location but not the content. We have live monitoring on Martin only a few times and only on my instruction, when he is doing something interesting.' He looked at his watch. 'Now I must go. You agree, Mr Thoroughgood, I have met my part of the bargain? Now you must give me yours.'

'You have met one part.'

'There is more? Only one was told to me.'

'We still need the chemical formula for Konyets.'

Sorokin shook his head. 'That was not part of the deal. That was the reason Martin gave to you for sending you to Russia. That is all. He never said so to me. He gave me his word of an English gentleman—'

'You didn't stop the killings after Martin agreed the deal. He understood you would. But you killed at least one other. That changed things. So we now need Konyets as well.'

Sorokin raised his voice. 'Please, Mr Thoroughgood, please, you listen to me. Assassinations are not in my control. Apart from Skripal, which was GRU blundering, they are decided and organised by the President's FSO. I have no control over the policy. But I control the agent who is doing it because he is one of ours. We trained him and provided him when they needed someone. I have ordered him to be withdrawn. We are waiting for message from him. We should have heard last night. Perhaps we did. I have been out of touch.'

'We need that formula.'

Sorokin raised his arms wide in simulacrum of helplessness. 'Please, please, I do not have it. How could I? It is nothing to do with my work.'

'You know people who have it. Get it from one of them.'

'This is not what Martin—'

'This is exactly what Martin would say if he were here.

I am saying it for him. Bring it to me tomorrow afternoon, when your conference finishes. Without it, no deal.'

There had been few occasions in Charles's career when he could play the uncompromising hard man. Usually, as the seeker after information he had to manoeuvre and negotiate, to wheel and deal. It was rare that he could insist. But when he could, as now, it was an easy part to play. Being uncompromising was always easy; it was compromise – effective compromise – that took hard thought and mental sweat. He already had what he most needed from Sorokin. The formula would be a bonus, possibly beyond Sorokin's reach, but there was no need to show that he understood that. As for the defection, he wouldn't think about that now. It was Martin's self-created problem and it was quite possible it would not be agreed. But getting the formula would help.

'But the plan,' said Sorokin, after a long pause. 'You tell me the plan?'

'The plan?'

'The exfiltration plan.'

'It's all in hand,' Charles lied. 'Provided you bring the formula.' So Martin had lied about that, too. Sorokin was clearly not expecting to have to come up with a plan himself. The only reasonable conclusion was that Martin had never intended to exfiltrate him, at least not yet. In which case, what did he intend? And if he did exfiltrate Sorokin, he'd have to come up with a source other than himself for the defectors' addresses, and trust Sorokin to support him. Not easy over months of patient debriefing. There was much that still didn't make sense.

They stared at each other for a few moments more, then Sorokin left the room, saying nothing. Charles stood at the window and watched him cross the road to the river, striding in the direction of the university. He tried to see if he could spot Tickeye picking him up but the only person to set off in his direction at his pace was a woman jogger in a blue tracksuit who had been sitting on a riverside bench. As he watched, his mobile vibrated in his pocket. The WhatsApp message from Sonia read, 'MM in Stockholm now believed on train to Uppsala.'

'How do you know?' Charles messaged back.

'Liaison monitoring his phone for us,' she replied.

So they had involved the Swedes. Fair enough, they were capable and secure. He looked out of the window again. Both Sorokin and the track-suited jogger were still in sight but this time he saw Tickeye following them at a distance. He messaged to tell him to leave Sorokin for now and go to the station and take on Manners. When he saw Tickeye turn back, he messaged again: 'MM did it. Used his phone in the office and when visiting defectors. They tracked him, got the addresses. He's trying to cover up, promising defection to S.'

CHAPTER TWELVE

They came for Dr Julia Andreyev when she was on her way home from work that evening. She had got off the bus and was walking towards her block, pondering whether she could be bothered to cook her *vareniki* with meat or whether she should use up the mushrooms. She did not notice the Mercedes drawing up behind her and disgorging two men wearing jeans, trainers and short dark jerkins. She did not see them until they were suddenly at her elbows, forcing her to stop.

'Come with us.'

One took her arm and led her back to the car, the other following. She felt mentally paralysed, she couldn't think, couldn't quite believe what was happening. They had put her in the middle of the back seat, one man on each side and the driver in front, before she managed a complete sentence. 'What is this? Why? Who are you? Where are you taking me?'

'You will see.'

They drove at pace towards the centre of St Petersburg. Familiar streets passed unregistered because behind her eyes was a seamless newsreel of images – her last conversation with Mikhail, the young woman in the hotel with the sign saying room 36, the grey-green eyes of the tweed-suited Englishman, herself tearing the Astoria price list with its pencilled alterations into little pieces before putting them inside an empty milk carton and dropping it in her waste-bin.

She had done that, hadn't she, not just imagined it? It wasn't still stuck there, incriminatingly, behind the gas stove? No, she had done it, as soon as she got back from seeing the Englishman. Her hands had trembled as she tore it into ever-smaller pieces. She had hardly slept that night and felt sick and shaky the next morning. She tried to tell herself she had done the right thing, she had not cooperated, had told them nothing. But she had also done a wrong thing by not telling the authorities. A big wrong thing. Did they know about it? Was this why she was in the car? She felt she was trembling again now, inwardly at least. Her breathing was shallow and rapid and she could feel her heart beating. The two men, sitting so tight against her that her arms were pinned to her ribs, must feel her shaking. But they showed no awareness, just sat staring straight ahead. Perhaps they were used to people shaking. Nobody spoke.

The building was old but clean, the lift silent; in the corridor she saw only men, some uniformed. The room they put her in was not a cell but felt like one, a barely furnished office with a brown metal desk and two plastic chairs, no pictures or ornaments. They held her by her upper arms and stood her in front of one of the chairs, facing the desk. She thought they were going to make her sit but they left her standing. Then they left the room, shutting the door.

She stood for some minutes. Tremors shot up and down her legs like electric currents. She wanted the loo. She would normally have gone when she got home, first thing. She was tempted to sit on the chair, but was afraid. Her chest felt tight.

The door was opened by a short balding man carrying a slim red file. He wore gold-rimmed glasses and a grey suit. He was about her age and his face was scrunched up like a wrinkled potato. He sat at the desk, opened the file and read the first typed page, without looking up at her. When he did he stared in silence for a few moments, the light from the window rendering his glasses opaque.

'You had a secret meeting with two English spies.'

She opened her mouth to speak.

'Say nothing unless I ask a question. You are here to answer questions.' He looked down at the file and turned the page. 'The English spies asked you for a secret chemical formula, the formula for Konyets.'

She nodded and swallowed.

'But you did not give it to them?'

'No. No.' She shook her head. At least they knew that. 'No, nothing. I gave them nothing.'

'Where is the formula?'

'At work. In my laboratory. We—'

The man took a black pen from his inside jacket pocket. 'Can you remember it?'

'No. Well, part of it, not all. It is not often necessary to refer to it in my work, I work with the substances.'

'If we take you to your laboratory now, will you be able to find it?'

She thought of her supervisor's desk. That was surely where it would be. It was not on any of their computer systems, at least not those she saw, but it must be available. People occasionally had to refer to it. It was no secret within the lab, since the lab itself and everything in it was secret. 'Yes, but you can get it, surely? You tell them you want it and they will give it to you. You are the—'

'*Organi*. Correct. We are the Organs of State Security.' There was no hint of a smile on the man's crumpled face. 'But sometimes it is necessary to do things secretly.' Those were his orders, telephoned by his boss in Uppsala: get the formula from the woman and make sure she tells no one. Her institution must never know that we wanted it, nor why. The man himself did not know why but he knew his boss and his own place in the organisation; he knew too that there were always wheels within wheels. It never paid to ask questions. 'We will take you there now and you will give it to us and then you can go home. You will tell no one about this. No one, ever. If you do, or if we only hear that someone has heard about it, we will recall that you were in

201

secret communication with agents of a foreign power and you will be arrested and tried and sentenced to the maximum. Remember this: we are the *organi*, we are always listening and we never forget.'

Julia nodded. She wanted to conform, to be obedient, to be accepted. She was loyal. She approved of everything that was regular and official. She would of course do what they said, would take them to the lab so that they could copy the formula. But this, though undoubtedly official because the *organi* were at the very heart of all that was official, was at the same time irregular. It undermined her institution, her department, it required her to do something against them, something that neither the Englishman nor even Mikhail had been able to persuade her to do. Yet the *organi* and her department were on the same side, she thought. It ought to be possible to do things in a regular manner.

She nodded again. 'Yes.' The pressure from her bladder was becoming intolerable and her chest was becoming tighter, making it difficult to breathe. 'May I please use the toilet?'

The man closed the file and stood. 'When you have given us the formula.'

Those were the last words Julia heard. The tightness in her chest suddenly intensified and expanded excruciatingly. It was as if everything inside her was twisted into a great knot. Then blackness and nothing. She had no last thoughts.

To her interrogator she appeared to be fainting. She swayed and went pale, her lips had a blueish tinge and her eyes seemed to widen as they fixed, unseeing, on his. Then she dropped her handbag and toppled backwards against the chair, knocking it over. She collapsed onto the brown lino with a prolonged crump and lay on her back, mouth and eyes open, legs apart, feet splayed. Her skirt had risen, displaying the insides of her thighs.

Her interrogator sat motionless while this happened, then got up and advanced tentatively from behind his desk, as if uncertain whether to help. When he saw that she was wetting herself, urine spreading across her crumpled skirt and the lino, he moved smartly to the door and shouted into the corridor. Then he picked up his file from the desk and stood holding it protectively against his chest with both hands.

Two uniformed guards appeared and stopped abruptly just inside the door, staring. 'Send for a doctor,' he said. 'Or a nurse.'

'Is she dead?' asked one.

'I don't know. Probably. It looks like it.'

'Has she fainted?'

'Maybe. Or maybe a heart attack. A doctor will know.'

One guard stepped cautiously forward, bending as if to check for a pulse.

'Don't worry about that now, just get a doctor,' said the interrogator before the guard could touch her. Then he left the room and hurried back down the corridor, his heels loud and rapid on the herringbone floor. He did not relish having to explain to his boss Colonel Sorokin that they had neither the formula nor – now – the means of getting it quickly and discreetly as the colonel required. He had no idea why the colonel wanted it; that was not his business. But it had been his business to get it, and he had failed. The fact that it was that stupid fearful woman who had failed him by having a heart attack would cut no ice with the colonel.

CHAPTER THIRTEEN

Feeling she had seen enough of the town for one morning, and longing to get her shoes off, Sarah returned to the hotel. On the way she lingered in the English Bookshop, settled on *Anna Karenina*, a book that for years she had been telling herself she ought to read. Then, as she approached the hotel, she remembered that they already had it at home in London, an old paperback copy of Charles's. Perhaps it was he who had said she should read it, all those years ago when they first knew each other, before her first marriage. Or perhaps it was her first husband. It was distressingly easy to muddle books and husbands.

If he wasn't still at his table in the bar, he would be closeted in their room with Sorokin, which would mean she couldn't go upstairs and change. He was not in the bar but fortunately his table, the one by the window, was free. She ordered coffee, tucked her feet beneath the chair and slipped her shoes off. Then she opened the book.

She had reached the point at which Karenin, returning home in his carriage, looks up to see his wife standing at an upstairs window, bare arms folded and head turned to an invisible presence behind her. At that point Sarah herself glanced out of the window. She thought afterwards that she must have been vestigially aware that someone was looking at her. But at the time she was not conscious of it and, even when she saw Martin Manners staring up at her from the pavement below, she did not immediately register that it was him. Her first perception was of an unshaven, grubby-looking man wearing a crumpled black raincoat and carrying a faded blue holdall. He was staring at her with a look of bafflement, his mouth open.

When she realised it was him she involuntarily raised her hand, smiling, then immediately thought she should not have, that he might be under cover and that she should therefore not recognise him. At first he simply stared back at her, not responding to her wave. She felt that there must be something wrong. He looked somehow odd, as if he was a character actor playing an older, run-down version of himself. She half rose from her seat, lopsidely feeling for her shoes beneath the chair. He continued to stare, then turned towards the hotel entrance. It wasn't immediately clear whether he was making for it or ignoring her. She got her shoes on after a brief ungainly struggle and left the table. They met as he climbed the stairs in the entrance.

'Hello, Martin.'

'Sarah.' He was panting, his red face creased in concern

as if she had given him bad news about herself. 'I didn't realise you were – no, I did, of course I did, of course – silly of me – suggested it myself – completely forgot . . .'

'Come in and have some coffee.'

She felt she sounded ridiculously artificial, as if they had run into each other in Fortnum & Mason or on Henley high street. But he followed her to the table. The barman came and took her order for two coffees. 'You look awfully tired, as if you could do with an infusion of caffeine.' She smiled.

Martin put his blue bag on the floor, stared at it for a few seconds, then looked out of the window. 'Not much sleep. None at all really, last night.'

'Worrying about making the early flight? I'm afraid I'm always like that.'

'Went straight to the airport. Waited there all night for it. Dozed a bit on the – you know – on the – on the seats.' He rested his arms on the table and stared at his clasped hands.

'Oh dear, did you have to? Couldn't you go home?' He was clearly not thinking straight. Perhaps a marital crisis on top of his other problems. She tried to think of some way to let Charles know, assuming Charles was still upstairs with Sorokin. She had manoeuvred Martin into sitting with his back to the reception area so that if they came down in the lift he wouldn't see them. 'You didn't go home, then?' she repeated. 'Are you going to stay here?'

He looked from the window to her as if he had forgotten she was there. 'Stay? Well, no – don't know. Yet. Find somewhere later. If I have to. Later. If I have to.'

'Tell me, Martin, what brings you here?' She spoke as if to a child. He stared at her and was still staring, disconcertingly, when the barman arrived with their coffees. 'Do you take milk?' she asked. He nodded. She poured. 'Sugar?' He shook his head. 'Perhaps I shouldn't have asked,' she said. It was possible he was ill or on medication, or something else.

'Asked what?'

'What brings you here.' He picked up his coffee and put it down, untasted. 'You don't have to tell me,' she continued, smiling. 'It's all right. I was just being nosy.'

'No, no, it's fine, it's fine.' He pulled a red-and-white spotted handkerchief from his trouser pocket and wiped his lips. 'No, I mean, better you than – you know – anyone else, really. Charles, of course. Have to tell Charles.' He put his handkerchief away and stared out of the window again.

'Tell him what?'

'About the colonel – Colonel Sorokin.'

'But he knows all about Sorokin. He's met him. You—'

'But he doesn't know that I . . . I . . . I can't get agreement, you see. Can't get it. To his defection. Not for weeks, maybe not ever. MI5 and the Home Office and the Foreign Office, they want me to – you know, explain everything, tell them how it happened. It was my phone, you see, they were monitoring my phone and – and getting the addresses of our defectors and then murdering them and Sorokin rang me and said he'd get it stopped if he could defect to us with his girlfriend and if not he'd let it be known that it was –

you know – my fault, my phone that they used to get the addresses. But when I tried to get MI5 to support the defection they – they wouldn't give a straight answer, said it would take time and they wanted to know the whole story. I'd have to tell them, you see, and – and people may not agree. So I've got to tell him, I've got to see him, Sorokin, and get him to – you know – stop the killings and hang on a bit. And maybe see if there's some other way without everyone knowing about my phone and all that.'

'But you've moved the surviving defectors, presumably given them new identities? Charles said that was the obvious—'

'That's happening, yes, but they'll still go on looking for them and we haven't caught their agent who's doing it. But I thought if I can get Sorokin to drop it in return for – for, you know, a debrief, debrief of me, a one-off, just enough to get him plenty of kudos with his own people, then we could forget about defection for the time being and it wouldn't all need to come out. The stuff about me, I mean. Then he and his girlfriend could defect later, maybe in a year or two.'

Sarah sipped her coffee, to give herself time. Martin's right leg, resting on the ball of his foot, vibrated beneath the table. He picked up his cup and put it down, again without drinking. She replaced her own cup carefully, with the tiniest chink against the saucer. 'A debrief, Martin? What does that mean?'

'Well, you know, a kind of – just a one-off – a kind of session with me in which he can ask whatever he wants. Something to make up for him not defecting yet. He'd get great credit in Moscow for it, probably promotion, and he could still defect later when everyone's . . . you know . . . forgotten about the defectors. Or at least it wouldn't be linked to it.'

Having been married to successive Chiefs, Sarah knew enough about the limits of acceptability to know that Martin was way out on his own in the stratosphere. 'Are you mad?' was what she wanted to say. Instead, she said, 'You mean, you'd let the Russians debrief you on what you know? Ask you who our agents are, that sort of thing?'

'Yes. Well, no, I mean there'd have to be some limits, obviously, but, you know, I could give them general guidance, that sort of thing. Might even be helpful to us both.' He stood abruptly. 'You don't know where it is, do you? I did know, read it somewhere. Can't remember now.'

'What – the gents?'

'The conference. Sorokin. I ought to find him. If I can speak to him soon I could get back today and no one will be any the wiser about my coming here.' He picked up his bag. 'Thanks for listening, Sarah. I feel much better about it with you and Charles onside. Thank you.'

Sarah stood. Perhaps he really was mad. At least, disengaged from reality, if that's what madness was. 'We're not, Martin,' she said firmly. 'We're not onside. Charles knows nothing about it and wouldn't dream of agreeing. He'd say you're crazy. Worse than crazy. He'd want you locked up. You mustn't do it, you really mustn't.'

His laugh was like a short bark. People at other tables looked round. 'Either that or I top myself. Can't bear for it all to come out. You do see that, don't you? Simply can't bear it. Charles will understand.' He stepped out from behind the table. 'Better get on. The university, isn't it – the conference? Remember now.' He glanced at his untouched coffee. 'Thanks for that, Sarah. Just what the doctor ordered. Which way is the university, the bit where the conference is?'

Sarah followed. 'No, wait; wait and see if I can get hold of Charles for you.'

'No time, must get on if I'm going to get back tonight. Say hello to him for me. He'll understand. Good man, your husband. Always was. Improvement on the first, anyway. Tell him I said so. Cheers.'

He strode out of the bar and hurried down the steps without waiting for directions.

Tickeye was on the bench on the other side of the road pretending to read a Danish paper. He had followed Martin from the Stockholm train and messaged Charles as they approached the hotel. Martin had at first seemed about to pass it but had then stopped and peered in through a window before entering. When he left a few minutes later and crossed the road towards the river, Tickeye folded his paper and followed at a distance.

Sarah, standing at her table and assuming Charles was still with Sorokin, messaged him and Tickeye telling them what Martin intended. 'Bonkers,' she concluded. 'Making no sense.' Tickeye had just acknowledged when Charles hurried downstairs. 'I didn't know he was here until I got your message. Tickeye sent one earlier but for some reason it only came through with yours. Which way did he go?'

Sarah pointed. 'Along the embankment towards the conference centre, though I don't think he realises it. Where's your colonel?'

'Heading that way himself. Could you ring Tickeye – ring, not message – and tell him from me that it's essential that Martin doesn't get to Sorokin. Shove him under a bus if necessary.'

'If you say that to Tickeye he probably will.'

'Well, a bike, then. Shove him under a bike. There's more of them anyway. I'll get hold of Sonia.'

Sonia was engaged. He left a message asking her to get the Stockholm station to ask Swedish liaison to help find and hold Martin on any pretext they could think of. 'Ring back and I'll explain,' he concluded.

Tickeye kept his phone in his hand after Sarah had spoken to him. Although he disliked them for his own use because they encouraged communication, they were a boon to watchers. They not only enabled real-time reporting without the complications of concealed radios, but they gave watchers something to be apparently doing while seemingly paying no attention to anyone.

He kept thirty to forty yards behind Martin, on the other side of the road. The shoals of cyclists were a convenient screen; if Martin looked back he wouldn't notice beyond them the short man engrossed in a phone conversation while staring across the river. But Martin did not look back. Carrying his blue holdall in his right hand, his left in his coat pocket, he walked rapidly but unevenly, occasionally lurching to one side as if to change direction, but then not. People would probably take him for a drunk, Tickeye reckoned, or for someone with a medical condition that interfered with motor skills. Twice he stopped to ask directions of people and each time they backed away as he spoke. He looked like a man not in full control of himself. That would make physical intervention easier, Tickeye thought. He could make it look as if he was helping. Having heard Sarah's summary of Martin's confession, he relished the prospect of physical intervention.

The conference centre was open to anyone although the hall itself was out of bounds to all but delegates. Martin arrived during a break in proceedings. Delegates were taking coffee and cakes in a section of the large foyer cordoned off by white plastic posts and pink rope. Tickeye followed him up the steps, dumping his newspaper in a bin and folding his black jerkin over his arm. He held his phone to his ear, nodding.

After a minute or two of wandering and lurching around the foyer, which Tickeye hoped might simplify matters by getting him thrown out, Martin gravitated towards the cordoned-off area. Tickeye closed in, still pretending to listen to his phone. Martin stood staring at the delegates. They were in groups, talking animatedly over their coffees and cakes. One or two noticed Martin, who looked as if he might be about to gatecrash and grab some cake, and turned their backs. He was obviously a problem for security to deal with. Tickeye regretted that he was not more formally dressed; he could have pretended he was security and escorted Martin out.

Martin made no move to enter the enclosure but continued to stand and stare, his hips against the pink rope. Then he walked slowly along the cordon, looking closely at the delegates. Most pretended not to notice. Tickeye kept parallel with him, occasionally glancing about as if having to think about something just said to him on his phone. Eventually Martin stopped beside a group of pale, dark-suited, middle-aged men on the other side of the rope. Unlike most other delegates, they did not avoid his eye but stared back at him, unabashed. When Tickeye saw him speaking to them he moved closer. He was sure the group was the Russian delegation but could not see Sorokin. There was no one tall enough.

Martin was speaking, his back turned towards Tickeye, who was not close enough to hear him. One of the delegates, a plump man nearest the rope, replied loudly in American-accented English. 'Yes, from Moscow and Petersburg. And you, from London?'

Martin spoke again. The plump man shook his head, looked at his colleagues, spoke in Russian, turned back and shook his head again. 'Colonel Sorokin is not here.'

Martin spoke again. 'In our hotel perhaps,' the man said,

adding, after another question, 'the Radisson. Maybe there, I don't know.' After another question from Martin he gave directions to the Radisson. 'And you – Mr? Mr Martin? You are his friend, yes? His friend from London?' He had another exchange in Russian with the others. 'We can take message for you. Tell me your business.'

Tickeye couldn't catch Martin's response and had to turn away when Martin left the group and meandered towards the exit. Tickeye followed. Three of the Russians were talking earnestly to the plump man, while the others watched Martin shamble away. A voice over the intercom announced in about half a dozen languages that the next session was starting. The Russians put down their coffees as one and moved off, except for the plump man, who took out his mobile and remained where he was.

Tickeye followed Martin out into the square. Unusually for him, he was unsure what to do. His task was clear enough: Manners was not to meet Sorokin. What he would do to prevent it he had yet to decide. It depended on the circumstances. His military experience had taught him that there were times when any decision was better than no decision. There were other times when it was best not to decide until you had to, when the reality of your options became clear. If they did.

He quickened his pace and put his black jerkin back on. He took a matching woollen hat from its pocket and pulled it down almost over his ears. Martin's shambling gait made it easy for Tickeye to skirt the edge of the square to position himself ahead. Martin changed direction twice and paused, swaying as if undecided or exhausted. Two passers-by slowed and stared as if to offer help, but moved on. Most gave him a wide berth. Tickeye decided. He turned and approached Martin head-on, hands in his jerkin pockets.

'Are you lost?'

Martin halted, puzzled, as if the voice had come from nowhere. It took him a second or two to focus, his mouth open, his red unshaven cheeks wobbling slightly. 'Yes, yes, I think I am.'

'Can I help?'

'Kind of you, most kind. Are you English, too? Everyone here speaks English.'

'I live here.'

'Yes, good. Very nice place. Don't blame you, don't blame you at all.' He stared. 'Don't I know you?'

Tickeye spoke gently. ''Course you know me, Martin. I used to be in the Office. Still am, now and again. You briefed me a while ago. And before that we were in the army together. But that was a long time ago.'

Martin nodded. 'The army, yes. I was in the army. You were too? We knew each other? Served together?'

When I was nobody and you were Golden Bollocks, Tickeye was tempted to say. Instead, he said, 'Where do you want to go, Martin?'

'I want – really, I want somewhere where nothing can . . . can . . .' He shook his head. 'The Radisson, that's what I'm after, what I'm looking for. Do you—?'

'I know it, I can take you there.'

'Straight across the square, someone said.'

'I'll take you there.' Tickeye offered his arm. 'Come on.'

Martin stared at the proffered arm. 'To be perfectly honest with you, I don't want – don't really want – I have to meet someone, you see.' He looked Tickeye in the eye, his gaze earnest, almost pleading. 'Meet someone. I'm going to meet someone.'

'There's a quicker way. By the river. A short cut. Come on.' Tickeye jigged his arm.

Martin took it, changing his holdall to the other hand. His grip was surprisingly strong but his hand shook. As they walked he became steadier, his speech became more coherent. 'Always liked Sweden. Scandinavia generally. Something in the genes, Viking ancestors, that sort of thing. What brings you here? Don't mind my asking?'

'I got married, years ago. Cranes now. I'm a crane operator. Travel all over but mainly Stockholm based.'

'Are you? Are you indeed? How fascinating.'

A crane conversation should see them through. It was an easy subject as it was a job he'd had after leaving the army. But while he spoke, keeping conversation going, Martin's hand heavy on his arm, he kept glancing at the puffy, vulnerable red face and asking himself whether he really had made his decision after all. There was still time to unmake it. But behind everything he saw in this hopeless, helpless face, beneath everything he heard in this tremulous voice still redolent with the accents of social assurance, was the knowledge that this once confident, now visibly crumbling, man had wrought the deaths of two of his agents. Two that he knew of. Maybe more. People he respected and felt responsible for. That made it personal.

'Down here,' he said, turning away from the road towards a quieter stretch of the river, every step taking them farther from the Radisson.

CHAPTER FOURTEEN

Charles sat by the window in their room that evening, waiting for Sorokin. The room was unlit so that he could see Sorokin arrive and check whether the Swedes were still on him. Presumably it wouldn't still be the female jogger, more likely cyclists. The Office would have to come clean with the Swedes about the whole case now, but that was up to the Stockholm station and Head Office, no longer his responsibility. His phone was on his lap, awaiting Tickeye's reply to his messages. He assumed he had prevented Martin from getting to Sorokin but it was odd to have no reply. For all his disdain of mobiles and communications in general, Tickeye was capable and prompt when forced to use them. Nor, according to Sonia's latest message, had the Swedes found Martin. They were still looking.

His phone buzzed but this time it was Sarah, downstairs in the bar with her book. She too was looking to see whether Sorokin was followed but the bar lights would make it difficult. 'Arrived' was all her message said. She would now go to the lift and swipe Sorokin in, travelling up with him as far as the floor below, without speaking.

Charles closed the curtains and turned on the lights. He put the door ajar and sat sideways to the shallow desk, notebook and pen before him. It was his late father's old fountain pen, a mottled 1920s Conway Stewart. He twiddled it on the desktop with his forefinger. It had travelled the world with him and had become familiar enough for him to no longer to think of it as special. It was a daily utensil, that was all, as it presumably had been for his father. And for his father before him. Any DNA attached to it could perhaps be read as family history, a history that would stop with him, there being no offspring to inherit. If only, he fancied, it could yield a read-out of every word it had written.

He was trying to empty his mind by twiddling. Impossible, of course, so long as consciousness remained, but it was something he tried to do before any difficult encounter. So long as he had thought it through in advance and was clear about what he wanted and what he would do if he didn't get it, he could mentally file it and pull it out when needed, confident it was all there. He stopped twiddling when he heard the lift.

Sorokin entered and closed the door carefully behind him. He remained just inside the door, hands in his Loden coat pockets. 'The formula. It was not possible. I do not have it.'

'Why not?'

'The source could not deliver.'

'Why not?'

'If you can wait maybe I get it for you later but not now. When I come out again.'

'When is that?'

Sorokin shrugged.

'So it's no deal.'

'We can still do deal if you can wait. So long as I know you will accept me in UK I can find other ways. It must be worth it for you, yes? You have important information already, Martin's telephone. So no more of your defectors will be killed.'

He made no move to advance into the room. Charles made no move to get up. 'Have you heard from Martin since we last met?'

Sorokin shook his head.

'Have you tried to contact him?'

'No. Why? I talk to you.'

It was of course possible that the defector subcommittee would accept him without the Konyets formula. He had yet to hear from Sonia about that. But it would be better with it. 'How likely is it that your source will deliver in the future?'

'Not likely. She is dead.'

'She?'

'Your Dr Julia, the woman who would not give it to you.'

'How did she—?'

'She died under interrogation.'

Charles imagined what might have been done to her.

Her face hovered in the room between them, perplexed and desperate as he had last seen it, an honest woman juggling loyalties. And his fault, at least in part. He should never have agreed to proposition her. 'You killed her? Your people.'

'My people did nothing. They picked her up and brought her in to explain what we wanted and she had heart attack, suddenly. She died straight away, on the floor. They say they did nothing to her. Not even shout. I believe them.'

There was no knowing whether to believe him. That was exactly what they would say, given that they understood Western sensitivities. Or squeamishness, as they would see it. He probably never would know.

'How will you get the formula now? You have another source?'

Sorokin nodded. 'The most straightforward is to ask through usual channels. We have the right and do not have to give reasons. But that would take time. If you give me time, it is certain. Other ways would be quicker but I would have to leave Russia immediately, the day after. You tell me which you want.'

If either, Charles thought. It may be that MI5 would be keen enough to talk to him regardless of Konyets, given what he must know about Russian UK sources, present and past. Konyets would be a bonus, not a qualifier. In which case there could be a message from Sonia or the Stockholm station within hours for him to exfiltrate Sorokin now, with or without girlfriend. 'Would you be prepared to defect now, without your girlfriend?'

'Yes.' Charles's face must have registered surprise because Sorokin added, 'It may be I am under suspicion because of that woman dying. People know about it but they don't know why I order it from abroad. They may suspect.'

'When do you return to Russia?'

'Tomorrow morning.'

'I will have an answer for you this evening. When will you be back in your hotel?'

'We have conference dinner with everybody. I have to be there but later I shall be in my room. You can call me.'

'Is that safe, on your phone? Your own people might be monitoring it already.'

Sorokin smiled for the first time. 'I am in charge of such things. I decide who is on the list.'

'But back in Russia there must be others who—'

He shook his head. 'I know what I am doing.'

Perhaps he did. On the whole agents understood their own bureaucracies better than their case officers. But they could be complacent, thinking they knew everything. There was, however, one threat he certainly didn't know about. 'I should warn you that Martin is here in Uppsala. He is looking for you.'

'He is here? Why?'

'I think he is having some sort of breakdown, a mental collapse. We're trying to find him but he's not answering his phone, the one you monitor. He thinks he can save his career by offering himself to you for a one-time debrief on everything he knows. In return for your not blackmailing him about the defectors his carelessness enabled you to kill.'

Sorokin's facial creases deepened. 'He is here, definitely here, now?'

'The danger is he'll approach you or people who know you in public. He's . . .' Charles hesitated. 'He's disturbed, his judgement is impaired. It may be better you don't go back to your hotel but go straight to wherever the conference dinner is and wait there. We're looking for him now. So are the Swedes.' He paused. Sorokin said nothing about having noticed surveillance. 'If we find him I'll call you, so you can relax. But until then, if you see him, flee.'

'Flee?'

'Run away, hide.'

Sorokin's expression was impossible to read now. He turned to go. 'One other thing,' said Charles. 'How did you know which room – which room in the Astoria – we were using?'

'That was easy.' Sorokin turned back. 'We monitor your room. You are not there. We look in the bar, restaurant, gym, lobby. You are not there. Then we look in the room of the girl from your embassy and find she is also not there. Now we are suspicious, we think you are doing something together. We switch on all the rooms of your delegation but you are not in any of them. So we switch on all the other rooms of the hotel that are booked, one by one, and soon we find you in number thirty-six, waiting for your visitor.' Sorokin shook his head, as to a child caught in some transparent misdemeanour. 'You are out of practice, Mr Thoroughgood.'

As soon as Sorokin left, Charles rang Sarah. 'On his way down. Anything from Tickeye?'

'Nothing.'

'Okay. I know he saw you on the way in, in the lift, but try not to let him see you now and follow him out if you can, just far enough to know where he's heading. I've told him not to go back to his hotel in case Martin's there. The Swedes may also be following him but don't worry about them.'

'Are you serious?' She laughed. 'I've never followed anyone in my life before. How close – hang on, the lift's here. Better go.'

Charles turned off the room lights again and stood by the window. It was properly dark now but he watched Sorokin's tall figure cross the road and head rapidly back towards the university area, parallel with the river. Seconds later Sarah followed, hurrying to keep up. If ever he operated in Uppsala again he'd hire a bike, he thought. You needed a bike to be anonymous. There was still no response from Tickeye. He messaged him again.

Sarah soon found herself panting to keep up. She was wearing moderately high heels and couldn't maintain the pace for long. She would go just far enough, she thought, to be sure whether he was heading for the conference centre or his hotel. He didn't once look round or about him, which was a blessing.

As neither did she. If she had she might have noticed she was not his only follower. There was a woman on a bike between them, pedalling slowly and pausing every so often to fiddle with her gears or lights. There was a man ahead of Sorokin walking fast enough to stay ahead and holding his phone to his ear. Behind her a VW Transporter van with Finnish registration crawled along, pausing every so often for a man to get out of the passenger door as if to check numbers on nearby buildings.

Sorokin seemed to be heading for the university area. If she could keep up the pace a little longer she would be able to say definitely. It was difficult because there were many busy bars and the pavement was crowded with students and bicycles. Sorokin seemed to cut through them without pause or deviation but she found herself constantly weaving and dodging. She lost sight altogether when he turned into a narrow road leading away from the river. She increased her pace as much as she could without quite breaking into a run, her shoes flapping against her heels. She didn't notice the man ahead of Sorokin turn round and walk rapidly back to the side road, nor the desultory cyclist suddenly speeding up and reaching it before the man. The VW Transporter accelerated past her to the junction and turned into it.

When she reached it she found a narrow road between two office buildings, neither with windows at ground-floor level. There was a 'No Exit' sign and the road became yet narrower after about fifty yards, where there was a street-lamp, beyond which was another lamp. She glimpsed bollards at the far end before a well-lit square but her view was cut off when the Transporter reached the narrowest part. Assuming Sorokin must be ahead of the van, she tried not to slow down, although her bunched toes were hurting with the effort to keep her shoes on. The van's brake lights came on and both doors opened. Two men got out and ran ahead of the van, out of her sight. She thought they must have run into something or someone. Perhaps they had run over Sorokin.

She was about twenty yards from the van when she heard a shout, then another. She stopped close to the right-hand wall, midway between streetlamps. A woman appeared from the other side of the van, opened the rear doors and stood holding one of them. Then the driver's door was pushed closed by the two men carrying or dragging something. A third man joined them and they struggled for a few moments, all three swaying and grappling. Then they started forward again to the back of the van. She saw now that they were wrestling with Sorokin. He was bent double with one man twisting one of his arms and another holding him in a headlock. The third man grabbed one of his legs and after another momentary swaying they heaved him face down into the back of the van. Two of the men followed and as the woman closed the doors on them, Sarah could see by the interior light that one was sitting on Sorokin's legs and the other kneeling on his neck and holding some sort of fastening. When the doors closed the third man got in the driver's door while the woman pushed the passenger door to and disappeared.

Sarah stood still, panting and feeling her heart pounding. The van's reversing lights came on and with a high-pitched whine it backed rapidly towards her. She flattened herself against the wall, fearful it would hit her yet at the same time worried about what the rough brickwork would do to her coat. The van came on, the wing mirror passing within inches of her nose. Then the dazzling headlights flooded the narrow road. It was impossible for her to see its number. As it reversed out onto the main road and disappeared, she glanced the other way in time to see a dismounted cyclist, a woman, pushing her bike in leisurely fashion between the bollards.

CHAPTER FIFTEEN

By the time Charles found somewhere to park near the canal, the evening had turned cold and wet. He picked his way along the unlit towpath, wary of the mooring ropes of the twenty or so narrow boats. His cap was down over his eyes and his tweed jacket buttoned against the wet gusts. He had no coat because the weather had been warmer and drier when he set off from Westminster, miscalculating the duration of the rush-hour but glad of the chance to exercise the Bristol. It had not been started since before the Swedish trip and he guiltily recalled his father's insistence that every car should be moved and run up to operating temperature at least once a week. Hunched against the gusts as he paused to make out the names of the boats, he wondered whether anyone ever really forgot the admonitions of childhood, whether or not they heeded them.

Now, sitting at the table in the warmth of Tickeye's cabin, the whisky bottle and the innocuous-looking white spray canister on the table between them, Charles was stuck for words. The lengthy pause had begun when he held up his hand and said, 'No, I do understand, I get it. I know what you mean. Just let me think.'

Not that there were many issues to think about. In fact, they were few and all too plain. The question was what to do about them, whether to do all that the law might demand, or as little as possible while keeping to its letter, or nothing at all. He was trying to convince himself that he would do whatever he truly believed was right.

But right in whose eyes? The law's? That could give only one answer, which meant full disclosure. In Sarah's eyes? He respected her opinion on ethical matters and although she might be prepared to stretch the law to its limits, she was conscientious and would never stray beyond them, which meant either full or at least partial disclosure. In Sonia's eyes? She would be more flexible, certainly when it came to manipulating internal procedures, but on an issue involving law and principle she would probably side with Sarah. He and he alone would consider option three. Which meant saying and doing nothing.

Tickeye rested his hand on the whisky bottle and raised his eyebrows. Charles shook his head. He had to drive back and there was no point in adding to the charge sheet. He already knew in his heart what he was going to do. The debate was within himself, finding a way to justify it. Tickeye poured.

'So you are telling me,' Charles resumed, 'that you last

saw the late Martin Manners walking along a deserted section of the riverfront in Uppsala and that you left him there, assuming he wasn't any longer looking for Sorokin.' He phrased it as a statement, not a question. Tickeye nodded. 'What did you think he was going to do?'

'Either nothing, just walk until he was tired out and then go home. Or top himself. Jump in the river. That's what I hoped he'd do. Do the decent thing.'

'And you are telling me that you didn't help him to jump, by persuasion or pushing.' Again, it was a statement and again Tickeye nodded. Martin's body had been spotted the following day by two boys fishing and subsequently identified by Swedish police. There were no signs of foul play. Not that Charles would have expected any if Tickeye had anything to do with it. 'So he either fell in while in a state of exhaustion or he drowned himself while temporarily of unsound mind?'

'Must've done.'

'Either way, you weren't there and you didn't push him.' Tickeye nodded.

'And then you walked back towards the town centre and while passing through the square near the conference centre you saw a figure you thought was Sorokin being grabbed behind the bollards in an adjoining road and hustled into a van which then reversed rapidly and disappeared. You couldn't see its number plate because of the headlights but you did see Sarah standing by the wall after it passed her.'

Tickeye nodded again, relaxed almost to the point of indifference. Charles had alerted Swedish liaison via Sonia as soon as Sarah returned and told him what had happened, which was before Tickeye reported. No trace of the Finnish-registered VW Transporter was found; CCTV did not show it subsequently being loaded onto any ferry nor was it spotted crossing the land border in the far north. Sorokin had not been seen or heard of again. Nor would he be now.

'All commendably straightforward,' Charles concluded, 'if perhaps not quite complete.' Tickeye shrugged, with the ghost of a smile. Charles sipped his whisky and nodded at the spray canister. 'Then there's this to be explained.'

'You know where I got it, I told you.'

'I know what you said. And I know what I think. And you know what I think too. But what do we want other people to know? Or think they know?'

'What they need to think they know is that one of Sorokin's kidnappers must have dropped it in the struggle. They were probably going to use it on him if they couldn't subdue him. I saw it rolling in the road behind the bollards as the van reversed. Sarah never saw it because she was behind the van when they grabbed him. I happened to be coming through the square when they grabbed him but couldn't make out everything that was going on because of the head-lights. After they reversed I followed and picked it up.'

'But you didn't report it to me when you came back to my hotel? And despite thinking it important enough to bring back, you haven't told anyone about it until telling me, now?'

'I didn't know whether it was anything important or just a bit of rubbish and didn't want to look stupid. Then I forgot about it. It was only when I heard more about how the defectors were probably killed by sprays that I thought it might be important.'

'And of course you still don't know whether it's important, whether it really is Konyets, and you won't until I've handed it in and Porton Down have analysed it and reported.'

Tickeye nodded, grinning openly this time. 'Sounds about right.'

'And praise is heaped upon you, Sonia and me.'

'Makes a change from shit.'

'So the secrets of Konyets are laid bare, there are no more defector murders, no high-level penetration of MI6, just a security lapse committed by a dead man. Serious in its consequences but there's nobody to blame, nobody living, anyway. So far so good. But what if he's found?'

'Who?'

Charles nodded again at the canister. 'The man from whom you really got this. Let's call him the donor.'

'He won't be. And if he ever is, there won't be anything to identify him.'

'It was murder, wasn't it?'

'Self-defence.'

'Keeping quiet about it makes me an accessory. Almost.'

'Not the first time, is it?' Tickeye raised his glass. 'Queen and country, and all that?'

Charles said nothing, then nodded. He raised his glass.